READING IN THE DARK

Seamus Deane was born in Derry in 1940. He has published a number of works of criticism and poetry and is the general editor of the *Field Day Anthology of Irish Writing*. He is currently teaching at the University of Notre Dame.

Seamus Deane

READING IN
THE DARK

V

VINTAGE

Published by Vintage 1997

15 17 19 20 18 16

First published in Great Britain by
Jonathan Cape Ltd, 1996

Vintage
Random House, 20 Vauxhall Bridge Road,
London SW1V 2SA

Random House Australia (Pty) Limited
20 Alfred Street, Milsons Point, Sydney,
New South Wales 2061, Australia

Random House New Zealand Limited
18 Poland Road, Glenfield,
Auckland 10, New Zealand

Random House (Pty) Limited
Endulini, 5a Jubilee Road, Parktown 2193, South Africa

The Random House Group Limited Reg. No. 954009
www.randomhouse.co.uk

A CIP catalogue record for this book
is available from the British Library

ISBN 0 09 974441 4

Printed and bound in Great Britain by
Cox & Wyman Ltd, Reading, Berkshire

The people were saying no two were e'er wed
But one had a sorrow that never was said.

'She Moved Through the Fair'

PART ONE

CHAPTER ONE

STAIRS

February 1945

On the stairs, there was a clear, plain silence.

It was a short staircase, fourteen steps in all, covered in lino from which the original pattern had been polished away to the point where it had the look of a faint memory. Eleven steps took you to the turn of the stairs where the cathedral and the sky always hung in the window frame. Three more steps took you on to the landing, about six feet long.

'Don't move,' my mother said from the landing. 'Don't cross that window.'

I was on the tenth step, she was on the landing. I could have touched her.

'There's something there between us. A shadow. Don't move.'

I had no intention. I was enthralled. But I could see no shadow.

'There's somebody there. Somebody unhappy. Go back down the stairs, son.'

I retreated one step. 'How'll you get down?'

'I'll stay a while and it will go away.'

'How do you know?'

'I'll feel it gone.'

'What if it doesn't go?'

'It always does. I'll not be long.'

I stood there, looking up at her. I loved her then. She was small and anxious, but without real fear.

'I'm sure I could walk up there to you, in two skips.'

'No, no. God knows. It's bad enough me feeling it; I don't want you to as well.'

'I don't mind feeling it. It's a bit like the smell of damp clothes, isn't it?'

5

She laughed. 'No, nothing like that. Don't talk yourself into believing it. Just go downstairs.'

I went down, excited, and sat at the range with its red heart fire and black lead dust. We were haunted! We had a ghost, even in the middle of the afternoon. I heard her moving upstairs. The house was all cobweb tremors. No matter where I walked, it yielded before me and settled behind me. She came down after a bit, looking white.

'Did you see anything?'

'No, nothing, nothing at all. It's just your old mother with her nerves. All imagination. There's nothing there.'

I was up at the window before she could say anything more, but there was nothing there. I stared into the moiling darkness. I heard the clock in the bedroom clicking and the wind breathing through the chimney, and saw the neutral glimmer on the banister vanish into my hand as I slid my fingers down. Four steps before the kitchen door, I felt someone behind me and turned to see a darkness leaving the window.

My mother was crying quietly at the fireside. I went in and sat on the floor beside her and stared into the redness locked behind the bars of the range.

DISAPPEARANCES

September 1945

People with green eyes were close to the fairies, we were told; they were just here for a little while, looking for a human child they could take away. If we ever met anyone with one green and one brown eye we were to cross ourselves, for that was a human child that had been taken over by the fairies. The brown eye was the sign it had been human. When it died, it would go into the fairy mounds that lay behind the Donegal mountains, not to heaven, purgatory, limbo or hell like the rest of us. These strange destinations excited me, especially when a priest came to the house of a dying person to give the last rites, the sacrament of Extreme Unction. That was to stop the person going to hell. Hell was a deep place. You fell into it, turning over and over in mid-air until the blackness sucked you into a great whirlpool of flames and you disappeared forever.

My sister Eilis was the eldest of the children in the family. She was two years older than Liam; Liam was next, two years older than me. Then the others came in one-year or two-year steps – Gerard, Eamon, Una, Deirdre. Eilis and Liam brought me to Duffy's Circus with them to see the famous Bamboozelem, a magician who did a disappearing act. The tent was so high that the support poles seemed to converge in the darkness beyond the trapeze lights. From the shadow of the benches, standing against the base of one of the rope-wrapped poles, I watched him in his high boots, top hat, candystriped trousers ballooning over his waist, and a red tailcoat of satin which he flipped up behind him at the applause, so that it seemed he was suddenly on fire, and then, as the black top hat came up again, as though he was suddenly extinguished. He pulled jewels and cards and rings and rabbits out of the air, out of his mouth, pockets, ears. When everything had stopped disappearing, he smiled at us behind his great moustache, swelled his candystripe belly, tipped his top hat, flicked his coat of flame and disappeared in a cloud of smoke and a bang that made us jump a foot in the air. But his moustache remained, smiling the wrong way up in mid-air, where he had been.

Everyone laughed and clapped. Then the moustache disappeared too. Everyone laughed harder. I stole a sidelong glance at Eilis and Liam. They were laughing. But were they at all sure of what had happened? Was Mr Bamboozelem all right? I looked up into the darkness, half-fearing I would see his boots and candystriped belly sailing up into the dark beyond the trapeze lights. Liam laughed and called me an eedjit. 'He went down a trapdoor,' he said. 'He's inside there,' he said, pointing at the platform that was being wheeled out by two men while a clown traipsed forlornly after them, holding Mr Bamboozelem's hat in his hand and brushing tears from his eyes. Everyone was laughing and clapping but I felt uneasy. How could they all be so sure?

EDDIE

November 1947

It was a fierce winter, that year. The snow covered the air-raid shelters. At night, from the stair window, the field was a white paradise of loneliness, and a starlit wind made the glass shake like loose, black water and the ice snore on the sill, while we slept, and the shadow watched.

The boiler burst that winter, and the water pierced the fire from behind. It expired in a plume of smoke and angry hissings. It was desolate. No water, no heat, hardly any money, Christmas coming. My father called in my uncles, my mother's brothers, to help him fix it. Three came – Dan, Tom, John. Tom was the prosperous one; he was a building contractor, and employed the others. He had a gold tooth and curly hair and wore a suit. Dan was skinny and toothless, his face folded around his mouth. John had a smoker's hoarse, medical laugh. As they worked, they talked, telling story upon story, and I knelt on a chair at the table, rocking it back and forth, listening. They had stories of gamblers, drinkers, hard men, con men, champion bricklayers, boxing matches, footballers, policemen, priests, hauntings, exorcisms, political killings. There were great events they returned to over and over, like the night of the big shoot-out at the distillery between the IRA and the police, when Uncle Eddie disappeared. That was in April, 1922. Eddie was my father's brother.

He had been seen years later in Chicago, said one.

In Melbourne, said another.

No, said Dan, he had died in the shoot-out, falling into the exploding vats of whiskey when the roof collapsed.

Certainly he had never returned, although my father would not speak of it at all. The uncles always dwelt on this story for a while, as if waiting for him to respond or intervene to say something decisive. But he never did. He'd either get up and go out to get some coal, or else he'd turn the conversation as fast as he could. It was always a disappointment to me. I wanted him to make the story his own and cut in on their talk. But he always took a back seat in the conversation, especially on that topic.

Then there was the story of the great exorcism that had, in one night, turned Father Browne's black hair white. The spirit belonged, they said, to a sailor whose wife had taken up with another man while he was away. On his return, she refused to live with him any more. So he took a room in the house opposite and stared across at his own former home every day, scarcely ever going out. Then he died. A week later, the lover was killed in a fall on the staircase. Within a year, the wife was found dead in the bedroom, a look of terror on her face. The windows of the house could not be opened and the staircase had a hot, rank smell that would lift the food from your stomach. Father Browne was the diocesan exorcist. When he was called in, they said, he tried four times before he could even get in the hall door, holding his crucifix before him and shouting in Latin. Once in, the great fight began. The house boomed as if it were made of tin. The priest outfaced the spirit on the stairs, driving it before him like a fading fire, and trapped it in the glass of the landing window. Then he dropped wax from a blessed candle on the snib. No one, he said, was ever to break that seal, which had to be renewed every month. And, he said, if anyone near death or in a state of mortal sin approached that window at night, they would see within it the stretched, enflamed face of a child in pain. It would sob and plead to be released from the devil that had entrapped it. But if the snib was broken open, the devil would enter the body of the person like a light, and that person would then be possessed and doomed forever.

You could never be up to the devil.

The boiler was fixed, and they went off – the great white winter piling up around the red fire again.

ACCIDENT

June 1948

One day the following summer I saw a boy from Blucher Street killed by a reversing lorry. He was standing at the rear wheel, ready to jump on the back when the lorry moved off. But the driver reversed suddenly, and the boy went under the wheel as the men at the street corner turned round and began shouting and running. It was too late. He lay there in the darkness under the truck, with his arm spread out and blood creeping out on all sides. The lorry driver collapsed, and the boy's mother appeared and looked and looked and then suddenly sat down as people came to stand in front of her and hide the awful sight.

I was standing on the parapet wall above Meenan's Park, only twenty yards away, and I could see the police car coming up the road from the barracks at the far end. Two policemen got out, and one of them bent down and looked under the lorry. He stood up and pushed his cap back on his head and rubbed his hands on his thighs. I think he felt sick. His distress reached me, airborne, like a smell; in a small vertigo, I sat down on the wall. The lorry seemed to lurch again. The second policeman had a notebook in his hand and he went round to each of the men who had been standing at the corner when it happened. They all turned their backs on him. Then the ambulance came.

For months, I kept seeing the lorry reversing, and Rory Hannaway's arm going out as he was wound under. Somebody told me that one of the policemen had vomited on the other side of the lorry. I felt the vertigo again on hearing this and, with it, pity for the man. But this seemed wrong; everyone hated the police, told us to stay away from them, that they were a bad lot. So I said nothing, especially as I

11

felt scarcely anything for Rory's mother or the lorry driver, both of whom I knew. No more than a year later, when we were hiding from police in a corn field after they had interrupted us chopping down a tree for the annual bonfire on the fifteenth of August, the Feast of the Assumption, Danny Green told me in detail how young Hannaway had been run over by a police car which had not even stopped. 'Bastards,' he said, shining the blade of his axe with wet grass. I tightened the hauling rope round my waist and said nothing; somehow this allayed the subtle sense of treachery I had felt from the start. As a result, I began to feel then a real sorrow for Rory's mother and for the driver who had never worked since. The yellow-green corn whistled as the police car slid past on the road below. It was dark before we brought the tree in, combing the back lanes clean with its nervous branches.

FEET

September 1948

The plastic tablecloth hung so far down that I could only
see their feet. But I could hear the noise and some of the
talk, although I was so crunched up that I could make out
very little of what they were saying. Besides, our collie dog,
Smoky, was whimpering; every time he quivered under his
fur, I became deaf to their words and alert to their noise.

Smoky had found me under the table when the room
filled with feet, standing at all angles, and he sloped through
them and came to huddle himself on me. He felt the dread
too. Una. My younger sister, Una. She was going to die
after they took her to the hospital. I could hear the clumping
of the feet of the ambulance men as they tried to manoeuvre
her on a stretcher down the stairs. They would have to lift
it high over the banister; the turn was too narrow. I had seen
the red handles of the stretcher when the glossy shoes of the
ambulance men appeared in the centre of the room. One
had been holding it, folded up, perpendicular, with the
handles on the ground beside his shiny black shoes, which
had a tiny redness in one toecap when he put the stretcher
handles on to the linoleum. The lino itself was so polished
that there were answering rednesses in it too, buried upside
down under the surface. That morning, Una had been so
hot that, pale and sweaty as she was, she had made me think
of sunken fires like these. Her eyes shone with pain and
pressure, inflated from the inside.

This was a new illness. I loved the names of the others –
diphtheria, scarlet fever or scarlatina, rubella, polio, influenza;
they made me think of Italian football players or racing
drivers or opera singers. Each had its own smell, especially
diphtheria: the disinfected sheets that hung over the bedroom

13

doors billowed out their acrid fragrances in the draughts that chilled your ankles on the stairs. The mumps, which came after the diphtheria, wasn't frightening; it couldn't be: the word was funny and everybody's face was swollen and looked as if it had been in a terrific fight. But this was a new sickness. Meningitis. It was a word you had to bite on to say it. It had a fright and a hiss in it. When I said it I could feel Una's eyes widening all the time and getting lighter as if helium were pumping into them from her brain. They would burst, I thought, unless they could find a way of getting all that pure helium pain out.

They were at the bottom of the stairs. All the feet moved that way. I could see my mother's brothers were there. I recognised Uncle Manus's brown shoes: the heels were worn down and he was moving back and forward a little. Uncle Dan and Uncle Tom had identical shoes, heavy and rimed with mud and cement, because they had come from the building site in Creggan. Dan's were dirtier, though, because Tom was the foreman. But they weren't good shoes. Dan put one knee up on a chair. There was scaffold oil on his socks. He must have been dipping putlocks in oil. Once he had invited me to reach right into the bucket to find a lock that had slipped to the bottom and when I drew it out, black to the upper muscle, the slick oil swarmed down my skin to corrugate on my wrist. I sprinkled handfuls of sawdust on it, turning my arm into a bright oatmeal sleeve that darkened before Dan made me wash it off.

But it was my mother's and father's feet that I watched most. She was wearing low heels that needed mending, and her feet were always swollen so that even from there I could see the shoe leather embedded, vanishing from that angle, into her ankles. There was more scuffle and noise and her feet disappeared into the hallway, after the stretcher, and she was cough-crying as my father's workboots followed close behind her, huge, with the laces thonged round the back. Then everybody went out, and the room was empty.

Smoky shook under his fur and whimpered when I

pushed him away. It was cold with all the doors open and the autumn air darkening. Una was going to die. She was only five, younger than me. I tried to imagine her not there. She would go to heaven, for sure. Wouldn't she miss us? What could you do in heaven, except smile? She had a great smile.

Everybody came in again. There wasn't much talking. My father stood near the table. I could smell the quayside on his dungarees, the aroma of horizons where ships grew to a speck and disappeared. Every day he went to work as an electrician's mate at the British Naval Base, I felt he was going out foreign, as we said about anyone who went abroad; and every day when he came back, I was relieved that he had changed his mind. Tom was pushing a spirit-level into a long leg-pocket of his American boiler-suit. Where would the little eye bubble of the spirit-level go now? Disappear into the wooden ends, go right off the little marked circle where it truly belonged? The circle would be big and empty. Dan picked up his coat, which had fallen off a chair on to the floor. I could see the dermatitis stains on his fingers and knuckles. He was allergic to the plaster he had to work with on the building site every day. Next month he'd be off work, his hands all scabs and sores. But Una would be long dead by then.

They all left except my parents. My father was at the table again. My mother was standing at the kitchen press, a couple of feet away, her shoes tight together, looking very small. She was still crying. My father's boots moved towards her until they were very close. He was saying something. Then he moved yet closer, almost stood on her shoes, which moved apart. One of his boots was between her feet. There was her shoe, then his boot, then her shoe, then his boot. I looked at Smoky, who licked my face. He was kissing her. She was still crying. Their feet shifted, and I thought she was going to fall, for one shoe came off the ground for a second. Then they steadied and just stood there. Everything was silent, and I scarcely breathed. Smoky crept out to sit at the fire.

That was my first death. When the priest tossed the first three shovelfuls of clay on to the coffin, the clattering sound seemed to ring all over the hillside graveyard, and my father's face moved sideways as if it had been struck. We were all lined up on the lip of the grave which was brown and narrow, so much so that the ropes they had looped through the coffin handles to lower it into the tight base came up stained with the dun earth. One of the gravediggers draped them over a headstone before he started pouring the great mound of clay in heaves and scrapes on top of the coffin. The clay came up to the brim, as though it were going to boil over. We subdued it with flowers and pressed our hands on it in farewell as we had pressed them on the glossy coffin top and on Una's waxen hands the night before at the wake, where one candle burned and no drink was taken. When we got back, the candle was out, and my mother was being comforted by aunts and neighbours who all wore the same serious and determined expression of compassion and sternness, so that even the handsome and the less-than-handsome all looked alike. The men doffed their caps and gazed into the distance. No one looked anyone else in the face, it seemed. The children appeared here and there, their faces at angles behind or between adults, fascinated, like angels staring into the light. I went up to the bedroom where Una had lain and sat on one bed and looked at hers and then buried my face in the pillow where her pain had been, wanting to cry and not crying, saying her name inside my head but not out loud, inhaling for something of her but only finding the scent of cotton, soap, of a life rinsed out and gone. When I heard noise on the stairs, I came out to see my uncles lifting the third bed from that downstairs room up over the banisters. They told me to stand aside as they worked it into the room and put it beside the bed where she had been sick. The wake bed was better; it had a headboard. Now Deirdre or Eilis would have one to herself.

Una came back only once, some weeks later, in early

October. My mother had asked me to visit the grave and put flowers on it. They would have to be wild flowers, since shop flowers were too expensive. I forgot until it was almost four o'clock and getting dark. I ran to the graveyard, hoping it would not be shut. But it was too late, the gates were padlocked. I cut up the lane alongside the east wall until I reached the corner where the wall had collapsed about two feet from the top. It was easy to climb over, and inside there was an untended area where the grass was long and where I had seen flowers growing before. But there was not a one, not even on the stunted hedgerow beneath the wall – not a berry, not a husk. I pulled some long grass and tried to plait it, but it was too wet and slippery. I threw the long stems away into the air that was already mottled with darkness, and they fell apart as they disappeared. Running between the little pathways that separated the graves, I got lost several times before I found the fresh grave and recognised the withered flowers as those we had left a short time before. I pulled the wreaths apart, hoping to find some flowers not so badly withered, but there were very few. A torn rose, a chrysanthemum as tightly closed as a nut, some irises that were merely damp stalks with a tinge of blue – that was all. But I couldn't get them to hold together with the bits of wire from the original wreaths, so I scooped at the ground and put them in a bunch together, pressing the earth round them with my foot. All the while, I was saying her name over and over. Una, Una, Una, Una, Una. It was dark, and I felt contrite and lonely, fearful as well. 'I have to go,' I said to the ground, 'I have to go. I don't like leaving you, but I have to go, Una.' The wall seemed far away. I got up off my knees and rubbed my hands on my socks. 'I'll come back soon.' I set off at a run, along the dark pathways, zig-zagging round headstones and great glass bells of airless flowers, Celtic crosses, raised statues, lonely, bare plots, another even fresher grave, where the flowers still had some colour even in the shrivelled light that made the trees come closer. She, it was Una, was coming right down the path before me for an

17

instant, dressed in her usual tartan skirt and jumper, her hair tied in ribbons, her smile sweeter than ever. Even as I said her name, she wasn't there, and I was running on, saying her name again, frightened now, until I reached the wall and looked back from the broken top stones over the gloomy hillside and its heavy burden of dead. Then I ran again until I reached the street lamps on the Lone Moor Road, and scraped the mud off my shoes against the kerb and brushed what I could of it from my clothes. I walked home slowly. I was late, but being a bit later did not matter now. I didn't know if I would tell or not; that depended on what I was asked. I knew it would upset my mother, but, then again, it might console her to think Una was still about, although I wished she wasn't wandering around that graveyard on her own.

My older brother, Liam, settled the issue for me. I met him in the street and told him instantly. At first he was amused, but he got angry when I wondered aloud if I should tell my mother.

'Are you out of your head, or what? You'd drive her mad. She's out of her mind anyway, sending you for flowers this time o' year. Sure any half-sane person would have said yes and done nothing. Anyway, you saw nothing. You say nothing. You're not safe to leave alone.'

All night, I lay thinking of her and hearing again the long wail of agony from my mother halfway through the family rosary. It made everybody stand up and Smoky crawl back under the table. I wished I could go in there with him but we all just stood there as she cried and pulled her hair and almost fought my father's consoling arms away. All her features were so stretched, I hardly recognised her. It was like standing in the wind at night, listening to her. She cried all night. Every so often, I would hear her wail, so desolate it seemed distant, and I thought of Una in the graveyard, standing under all those towering stone crosses, her ribbons red.

READING IN THE DARK

October 1948

The first novel I read had a green hardboard cover and was two hundred and sixteen pages long. On the flyleaf my mother had written her maiden name. I stared at it. The ink had faded, but the letters were very clear. They seemed strange to me, as though they represented someone she was before she was the mother I knew, who might not even have been the same person who wrote the shopping lists and counted up the grocer's book every week and rolled her eyes and said what I took to be prayers and aspirations under her breath. Underneath her name, she had written *Eucharistic Congress, Dublin, 1932*. I didn't know what a Eucharistic Congress was, and when I asked the answers seemed very vague. They all seemed to be about St Patrick and a Count John McCormack, who sang a hymn called 'Panis Angelicus' over and over again, for most of 1932 as far as I could understand.

The novel was called *The Shan Van Vocht*, a phonetic rendering of an Irish phrase meaning The Poor Old Woman, a traditional name for Ireland. It was about the great rebellion of 1798, the source of almost half the songs we sang around the August bonfires on the Feast of the Assumption. In the opening pages, people were talking in whispers about the dangers of the rebellion as they sat around a great open-hearth fire on a wild night of winter rain and squall. I read and re-read the opening many times. Outside was the bad weather; inside was the fire, implied danger, a love relationship. There was something exquisite in this blend, as I lay in bed reading while my brothers slept and shifted under the light that shone on their eyelids and made their dreams different. The heroine was called Ann, and the hero was

19

Robert. She was too good for him. When they whispered, she did all the interesting talking. He just kept on about dying and remembering her always, even when she was there in front of him with her dark hair and her deep golden-brown eyes and her olive skin. So I talked to her instead and told her how beautiful she was and how I wouldn't go out on the rebellion at all but just sit there and whisper in her ear and let her know that now was forever and not some time in the future when the shooting and the hacking would be over, when what was left of life would be spent listening to the night wind wailing on graveyards and empty hillsides.

'For Christ's sake, put off that light. You're not even reading, you blank gom.'

And Liam would turn over, driving his knees up into my back and muttering curses under his breath. I'd switch off the light, get back in bed, and lie there, the book still open, re-imagining all I had read, the various ways the plot might unravel, the novel opening into endless possibilities in the dark.

The English teacher read out a model essay which had been, to our surprise, written by a country boy. It was an account of his mother setting the table for the evening meal and then waiting with him until his father came in from the fields. She put out a blue-and-white jug full of milk and a covered dish of potatoes in their jackets and a red-rimmed butter dish with a slab of butter, the shape of a swan dipping its head imprinted on its surface. That was the meal. Everything was so simple, especially the way they waited. She sat with her hands in her lap and talked to him about someone up the road who had had an airmail letter from America. She told him that his father would be tired, but, tired as he was, he wouldn't be without a smile before he washed himself and he wouldn't be so without his manners to forget to say grace before they ate and that he, the boy, should watch the way the father would smile when the books were produced for homework, for learning was a wonder to him, especially the Latin. Then there would be no talking, just the ticking of the clock and the kettle humming and the china dogs on the mantelpiece looking, as ever, across at one another.

'Now that,' said the master, 'that's writing. That's just telling the truth.'

I felt embarrassed because my own essay had been full of long or strange words I had found in the dictionary – 'cerulean', 'azure', 'phantasm' and 'implacable' – all of them describing skies and seas I had seen only with the Ann of the novel. I'd never thought such stuff was worth writing about. It was ordinary life – no rebellions or love affairs or dangerous flights across the hills at night. And yet I kept remembering that mother and son waiting in the Dutch interior of that essay, with the jug of milk and the butter on the table, while behind and above them were those wispy, shawly figures from the rebellion, sibilant above the great fire and below the aching, high wind.

GRANDFATHER

December 1948

Brother Regan was lighting a candle in his dark classroom at the foot of the statue of the Blessed Virgin. Regan permitted no overhead lights when he gave his Christmas address in primary school. Regan was small, neat, economical. He had been at Una's funeral earlier that year, along with several other Christian Brothers from the primary school.

'Boys,' he said.

After he said 'Boys', he stopped for a bit and looked at us. Then he dropped his eyes and kept them down until he said, more loudly again,

'*Boys.*'

He had complete silence this time.

'Some of you here, one or two of you, perhaps, know the man I am going to talk about today. You may not know you know him, but that doesn't matter.

'More than twenty-five years ago, during the troubles in Derry, this man was arrested and charged with the murder of a policeman. The policeman had been walking home one night over Craigavon Bridge. It was a bleak night, November, nineteen hundred and twenty-one. The time was two in the morning. The policeman was off duty; he was wearing civilian clothes. There were two men coming the other way, on the other side of the bridge. As the policeman neared the middle of the bridge, these two men crossed over to his side. They were strolling, talking casually. They had their hats pulled down over their faces and their coat collars turned up for it was wet and cold. As they passed the policeman, one of them said, "Goodnight," and the policeman returned the greeting. And then suddenly he found himself grabbed from behind and lifted off his feet. He tried to kick but one

22

of the men held his legs. "This is for Neil McLaughlin," said one. "May you rot in the hell you're going to, you murdering . . . " '

Regan shook his head rather than say a swear word. Then he went on.

'They lifted him to the parapet and held him there for a minute like a log and let him stare down at the water — seventy, eighty feet below. Then they pushed him over and he fell, with the street lights shining on his wet coat until he disappeared into the shadows with a splash. They heard him thrashing, and he shouted once. Then he went under. His body was washed up three days later. No one saw his assailants.

'They went home and said nothing. A week later, a man was arrested and charged with the murder. He was brought to trial. But the only evidence the police had was that he was the friend and workmate of Neil McLaughlin, who had been murdered by a policeman a month before. The story was that, before McLaughlin died on the street where he had been shot, coming out of the newspaper office where he worked, he had whispered the name of his killer to this man who had been arrested. And this man had been heard to swear revenge, to get the policeman — let's call him Billy Mahon — in revenge for his friend's death. There was no point in going to the law, of course, justice would never be done; everyone knew that, especially in those early years. So maybe the police thought they could beat an admission out of him, but he did not flinch from his story. That night, he was not even in the city. He had been sent by his newspaper to Letterkenny, twenty miles away, and he had several witnesses to prove it. The case was thrown out. People were surprised, even though they believed the man to be innocent. Innocence was no guarantee for a Catholic then. Nor is it now.

'Well, I wasn't even in the city in those days. But one of the priests, with whom I have since become friends, was then a young curate. He told me the story of the accused

23

man. This man was prominent in local sporting circles and he helped in various ways to raise money for the parish building fund. One night, in the sacristy of the Long Tower Church, just down the road from here, he told the priest that he had not been to confession in twenty years. He had something on his conscience that no penance could relieve. The priest told him to trust in God's infinite mercy. He offered to hear the man's confession; he offered to find someone else, a monk he knew down in Portglenone, to whom the man could go, in case he did not want to confess to someone he knew. But no, he wouldn't go. No penance, he said, would be any use, because, in his heart, he could not feel sorrow for what he had done. But he wanted to tell someone, not as a confession, but in confidence.

'So he told the priest about being arrested. He told him about the beatings he had been given – rubber truncheons, punches, kicks, threats to put him over the bridge. He told how he had resisted these assaults and never wavered.

'The priest told him that such steadiness in sticking to his story was a testimony to the strength a person gets from knowing he is in the right.

'He looked at the priest in amazement. And then he said these words, words the priest never forgot.

' "D'ye think that's what I wanted to tell you? The story of my innocence? For God's sake, Father, can't you see? I wasn't innocent. I was guilty. I killed Mahon and I'd kill him again if he came through the door this minute. That's why I can't confess. I have no sorrow, no resolve not to do it again. No pity. Mahon shot my best friend dead in the street, for nothing. He was a drunken policeman with a gun, looking for a Catholic to kill, and he left that man's wife with two young children and would have got off scot-free for the rest of his days; probably got promoted for sterling service. And Neil told me as he lay there, with the blood draining from him, that Mahon did it. 'Billy Mahon, Billy Mahon, the policeman,' that's what he said. And even then I had to run back into the doorway and leave his body

24

there in the street because they started shooting down the street from the city walls. And I'm not sorry I got Mahon and I told him what it was for before I threw him over that bridge and he knew, just too late, who I was when I said goodnight to him. It was goodnight all right. One murdering . . . " ' – Regan bowed his head – ' "less."

'Boys, in the story the priest told to me, and that I have now just told to you, look what happened. A man went to the grave without confessing his sin. And think of all the things that were done in that incident. The whole situation makes men evil. Evil men make the whole situation. And these days, similar things occur. Some of you boys may feel like getting involved when you leave school, because you sincerely believe you will be on the side of justice, fighting for the truth. But, boys, let me tell you, there is a judge who sees all, knows all and is never unjust; there is a judge whose punishments and rewards are beyond the range of human imagining; there is a Law greater than the laws of human justice, far greater than the law of revenge, more enduring than the laws of any state whatsoever. That judge is God, that Law is God's Law, and the issue at stake is your immortal soul.

'We live, boys, in a world that will pass away. The shadows that candle throws upon the walls of this room are as insubstantial as we are. Injustice, tyranny, freedom, national independence are realities that will fade too, for they are not ultimate realities, and the only life worth living is a life lived in the light of the ultimate. I know there are some who believe that the poor man who committed that murder was justified, and that he will be forgiven by an all-merciful God for what he did. That may be. I fervently hope that it is so, for who would judge God's mercy? But it is true, too, of the policeman: he may have been as plagued by guilt as his own murderer; he may have justified himself too; he may have refused sorrow and known no peace of mind; he may have forgiven himself or he may have been forgiven by God. It is not for us to judge. But it is for us to distinguish, to see the difference between wrong done to us and equal wrong done *by* us; to know that our transient life, no matter how scarred, how broken, how miserable it may be, is also God's miracle and gift; that we may try to improve it, but we may not destroy it. If we destroy it in another, we destroy it in ourselves. Boys, as you leave another year behind, you come that much closer to entering a world of wrong, insult, injury, unemployment, a world where the unjust hold power and the ignorant rule. But there is an inner peace nothing can reach; no insult can violate, no corruption can deprave. Hold to that; it is what your childish innocence once was and what your adult maturity must become. Hold to that. I bless you all.'

And he raised his hand and made the sign of the Cross above our heads and crossed the room, blew out the candle as the bell rang wildly in the chapel tower, and asked that the lights be switched on. He left in silence with the candle smoking heavily behind him at the foot of the statue, stubby in its thick drapery of wax.

'That was your grandfather,' said McShane to me. 'I know that story too. He worked at the newspaper office and he was McLaughlin's friend. My father told me all about it.'

I derided him. I had heard the story too, but I wasn't going to take it on before everyone else. Not if my mother's father was involved. Did Regan know? Was it really my grandfather who had done that, the little man who sat around in his simmet vest all day long, looking sick and scarcely saying a word? Anyway, it was just folklore. I had heard something of it when I was much younger and lay on the landing at night listening to the grown-ups talking in the kitchen below and had leaned over the banisters and imagined it was the edge of the parapet and that I was falling, falling down to the river of the hallway, as deaf and shining as a log.

PISTOL

January 1949

In that dark winter, there were two police cars, black and black, that appeared to have landed like spaceships out of the early morning light of the street. I saw their gleaming metal reflected in the lacquered window glass of the house next door as they took off with us. But first there was the search. A bright figure, in a white rain-cape, came through the bedroom door and stood with his back to the wall, switching the light on and off. He was shouting, but I was numb with shock and could see only his mouth opening and closing. I dressed within that thin membrane of silence. They were, I knew, looking for the gun I had found the afternoon before in the bottom drawer inside the wardrobe of the room next door, where my sisters slept.

It was a long, chill pistol, blue-black and heavy, which I had smuggled out the back to show to some boys from Fahan Street, up near the old city walls. They had come over to play football and afterwards we had an argument about politics. I had been warned never even to mention the gun which, I was told, had been a gift to my father from a young German sailor, whose submarine had been brought in to the port at the end of the war. He had been held with about thirty others in Nissen huts down by the docks, and my father used to bring him extra sandwiches or milk every lunch-time when he was helping to wire up the huts for light and heat. Before he went away the young sailor gave my father the gun as a memento. But since we had cousins in gaol for being in the IRA, we were a marked family and had to be careful. Young as I was, I was being stupid.

While we were gathered round the gun, hefting it, aiming it, measuring its length against our forearms, I had felt eyes watching. Fogey McKeever, known to be a police informer, was at the end of the lane, looking on. He was a young, open-faced man of twenty or so with a bright smile and wide-spaced, rounded eyes. He looked the soul of candour. He had seen me bring the gun back into the house.

I waited ten minutes and then brought it out again, wrapped in an old newspaper, and buried it in one of the stone trenches up the field. I was so sure that was enough that I had forgotten about it even before I went to sleep. But now, here were the police, and the house was being splintered open. The linoleum was being ripped off, the floorboards crowbarred up, the wardrobe was lying face down in the middle of the floor and the slashed wallpaper was hanging down in ribbons.

We were huddled downstairs and held in the centre of the room while the kitchen was searched. One policeman opened a tin of Australian peaches and poured the yellow scimitar slices and the sugar-logged syrup all over the floor. Another went out to the yard and split open a bag of cement in his ransack of the shed. He came walking through in a white cloud, his boots sticking to the slimy lino and the cement falling from him in white flakes. I was still in the silence. Objects seemed to be floating, free of gravity, all over the room. Everybody had sweat or tears on their faces. Then my father, Liam and I were in the police cars and the morning light had already reached the roof-tops as a polished gleam in the slates that fled as we turned the corner of the street towards the police barracks, no more than a few hundred yards away.

Where was the gun? I had had it, I had been seen with it, where was it? Policemen with huge faces bent down to ask me, quietly at first, then more and more loudly. They made my father sit at a table and then lean over it, with his arms outspread. Then they beat him on the neck and shoulders with rubber truncheons, short and gorged-red in colour. He told them, but they didn't believe him. So they beat us too, Liam and me, across the table from him. I

28

remember the sweat and rage on his face as he looked. When they pushed my chin down on the table for a moment, I was looking up at him. Did he wink at me? Or were there tears in his eyes? Then my head bounced so hard on the table with the blows that I bit hard on my tongue.

For long after, I would come awake in the small hours of the morning, sweating, asking myself over and over, 'Where is the gun? Where is it? Where is the gun?' I would rub the sleep and fear that lay like a cobweb across my face. If a light flickered from the street beyond, the image of the police car would reappear and my hair would feel starched and my hands sweaty. The police smell took the oxygen out of the air and left me sitting there, with my chest heaving.

CHAPTER TWO

FIRE

June 1949

It was a city of bonfires. The Protestants had more than we had. They had the twelfth of July, when they celebrated the triumph of Protestant armies at the Battle of the Boyne in 1690; then they had the twelfth of August when they celebrated the liberation of the city from a besieging Catholic army in 1689; then they had the burning of Lundy's effigy on the eighteenth of December. Lundy had been the traitor who had tried to open the gates of the city to the Catholic enemy. We had only the fifteenth of August bonfires; it was a church festival but we made it into a political one as well, to answer the fires of the twelfth. But our celebrations were not official, like the Protestant ones. The police would sometimes make us put out the fires or try to stop us collecting old car tyres or chopping down trees in preparation. Fire was what I loved to hear of and to see. It transformed the grey air and streets, excited and exciting. When, in mid-August, to commemorate the Feast of the Assumption of Our Lady into heaven, the bonfires were lit at the foot of the sloping, parallel streets, against the stone wall above the Park, the night sky reddened around the rising furls of black tyre-smoke that exploded every so often in high soprano bursts of paraffined flame. Their acrid odour would gradually give way to the more fragrant aroma of soft-burning trees that drifted across the little houses in their serried slopes, gravelled streets falling down from the asphalted Lone Moor Road that for us marked the limit between the city proper and the beginning of the countryside that spread out into Donegal four miles away. In the small hours of the morning, people sitting on benches and kitchen chairs around the fire were still singing; sometimes a window in one of the nearby houses cracked in a spasm of heat; the police car, that had been sitting in the outer darkness of two hundred yards away, switched on its lights and glided away; the shadows on the gable wall shrivelled as the fires burnt down to their red intestines. The Feast of the Assumption dwindled into the sixteenth of August, and solo singers began to dominate the sing-along chorusing. It marked the end of summer. The faint bronze tints of the dawn implied autumn, and the stars fainted into the increasing light as people trailed their chairs reluctantly home.

The dismembered streets lay strewn all around the ruined distillery where Uncle Eddie had fought, aching with a long, dolorous absence. With the distillery had gone the smell of vaporised whiskey and heated red brick, the sullen glow that must have loomed over the crouching houses like an amber sunset. Now, instead, we had the high Gothic cathedral and its parochial house, standing above the area in a permanent greystone winter overlooking the abandoned site that seemed to me a faithless and desolate patch, rinsed of its colour, pale and bald in the midst of the tumble of small houses, unpaved streets and the giant moraine of debris that had slid from the foot of the city walls down a sloping embankment to where our territory began. In the early winter evenings, people angled past like shadows under the weak street lights, voices would say goodnight and be gone.

There were two open spaces near our house. Behind our row of houses, the back field sloped up towards the Lone Moor Road; it ended in a roadway that curved down towards Blucher Street and then straightened towards the police barracks, three hundred yards away. The roadway was flanked by a stone wall, with a flat parapet, only five feet high on our side, twelve feet high on the other. On the other side was Meenan's Park, although the older people still called it Watt's Field, after the owner of the distillery. We could climb the wall and drop down on the other side; but the wall ran past the foot of the streets — Limewood, Tyrconnell,

Beechwood and Elmwood – pierced by a rectangular opening at each street that led to a flight of railed steps down to the park. A line of air-raid shelters separated the top section of the park from the open spaces beyond, where we played football. At night, the field and the park were pitch-black. The only street lighting was a single curved lamp, eight feet high, at the end of each street. We were told never to play in the park at night, for Daddy Watt's ghost haunted it, looking for revenge for the distillery fire that had ruined him. Those who saw him said he was just a black shape that moved like a shadow around the park, but that the shape had a mouth that opened and showed a red fire raging within.

To reach the ruins of the distillery, we had only to cross Blucher Street, go along Eglinton Terrace, across the mouth of the Bogside, with the city abattoir on our left, the street stained by the droppings of the cows, pigs and sheep that were herded in there from the high lorries with their slatted sides. There, vast and red-bricked, blackened and gaunt, was the distillery, taking up a whole block of territory. The black stumps of its roof-timbers poked into the sky. Sometimes, when passing there, I would hear the terrified squealing of pigs from the slaughterhouse. They sounded so human I imagined they were going to break into words, screaming for mercy. And the noise would echo in the hollow distillery, wailing through the collapsed floors, clinging to the blackened brick inside. I had heard that people ran from their houses as the shooting started and the police cordon tightened. The crowd in the street, at the top of the Bogside, started singing rebel songs, but the police fired over their heads and the crowd scattered. The IRA gunmen, on the roof or at the top-floor windows, fired single shots, each one like a match flare against the sky. They were outgunned, surrounded, lost. It was their last-minute protest at the founding of the new state. Then the explosion came and the whole building shook and went on fire. No one knew when or if the building would be repaired or knocked down and replaced. It was a burnt space in the heart of the neighbourhood.

The town lay entranced, embraced by the great sleeping light of the river and the green beyond of the border. It woke now and then, like someone startled and shouting from a dream, in clamour at its abandonment. Once, at the height of a St Patrick's Day riot, when the police had baton-charged a march and pursued us into our territory, we enticed them to follow us further downhill from the Lone Moor into the long street called Stanley's Walk that ran parallel with our own. We had splashed half a barrel of oil from a ransacked garage on the road surface at the curve of the slope. The police and B Specials raced down after us, under a hail of stones thrown at the cars and the jeeps they rode in or ran alongside. Advertising hoardings at the side of the street took the first volley of our missiles as the two leading cars hit the oil. A giant paper Coca-Cola bottle was punctured, along with the raised chin of a clean-shaven Gillette model. The cars swung and hurtled into the side walls, shredding stones from them like flakes of straw. The oil glittered in the sudsy swathe of the tyres, and one car lit up in a blue circle of flame as the police ran from it. The whole street seemed to be bent sideways, tilted by the blazing hoardings into the old Gaelic football ground.

AMERICAN CITIES

September 1949

Chicago was a place I longed to see. I had heard that there had been a big fire there once, although I wondered if that were not a mix-up with San Francisco and the earthquake that I knew had destroyed it. American cities were given to catastrophe. 'The British bombed Washington,' Uncle Dan told me. Was this also part of the war? I imagined Spitfires, with their red, white and blue bull's-eyes on the wings, zooming down, the way the Germans zoomed down on us, and the Americans shouting 'Goddamn'. 'They never did,' said Uncle Manus. 'Bombed it flat,' said Dan, 'I'm tellin' you. They did so. I read that somewhere.' All those American cities destroyed – bombs, fire, earthquake. It was hard to imagine. Dan said that someone he knew had seen the Chicago fire and had said it leapt across the river like an animal, and that the water steamed. John said he'd seen the whiskey running in the gutters after the distillery fire, with the flames running along the top in a blue fringe, and people collecting it in buckets. There were bullets whizzing everywhere. One of them had knocked the bucket from a man's hand, and the whiskey had exploded and the man had shouted curses at the IRA men for losing him his whiskey and ruining a good bucket. Oh, that was only a wee fire compared to what we have now, said the others. Sure there's parts of Germany and Russia that, they say, will still be smouldering by the end of the century. People just evaporated in the heat. 'Can you evaporate?' I asked my father. He thought so. Jesus Christ, I wish they'd drop one or two of those evaporator bombs in this Godforsaken hole, said Dan; at least we'd feel a bit of heat once before we go into the Big Blue Yonder. He always said that. The Big Blue Yonder.

Armies went into it. Warships were blown up into it. Submarines were felled below the water and spun downward into it. Cities, blurred by bombing, faded into it. I could see the American cities sailing into that Yonder, their skyscraper heads flaring under the clouds, especially after someone said that the city of Los Angeles meant the City of the Angels. That made its rising from the earth to the sky seem more likely. Some angels, those boyos over there, said Tom. The wildness of Dan's Yonder seemed to fit in with American cities and their spectacular destinies. With us, there was just the enclosing rain, so fine that they said there was no space between the lines of it except for someone like Dan who was so skinny he could wriggle through it for an hour and still be dry as a bone. It was only when he put a coat on that you could see him. Dan laughed and claimed that compared to my aunt Katie's husband, Tony McIlhenny, he was at least a string with knots in it. McIlhenny's ears, he said, were wider than his shoulders. You're not to mention that bastard, said Manus; skinny an'all as he was, he did enough damage for ten men. Didn't he go to Chicago? I asked. They all turned round and looked at me. Ay, he did, said one of them. An' didn't come back either. Left his wife and wee'un. Never trusted him myself. Too much the charmer, always the ladies' man. Looked like an Italian, didn't he? asked another. Talked like one too, with his arms waving and that big smile on his face. Oh, a real rare one, McIlhenny. Didn't he see Eddie in Chicago? I asked again; didn't he write home to Katie to say he did? That's a fact, said Manus. He did so. Maybe Eddie had died in the big fire there in Chicago, said John. Escaped one here, was got by another there. What do you think, Frank? Not at all, my father replied. That Chicago fire; that was long before Eddie got there. If he ever did, someone said. Are you sure of those dates? Wasn't it about the same time? Their voices chorused back and forth. If he ever did. I couldn't remember which one of them said that. And if he didn't? Why did McIlhenny not come back or at least send for his wife and child? Those skyscrapers in Chicago are so high, said Dan, you could drink a bottle of whiskey on the top floor and you'd have a hangover before you were halfway down – even if you used a parachute. They all laughed and cut the cards again, dealing them out rapidly as they chuckled, 'Jack high, you've the shout,' 'Three to a run,' 'Two pair.' I left to play handball at the gable wall of the house at the end of the street. I'd dodge between the strokes of the rain and come home dry as you like after they had all gone, and my father would be nodding off to sleep in his chair with the cards scattered all over the table, their blacks and reds shining.

BLOOD

October 1949

She coughed. Crimson sparks landed all over her grey night-dress and the bedclothes. She looked at me, her eyes wide. I couldn't move, my legs were so leaden and a pulse passed up and down from my head to my toes as though someone had slashed me from behind. Before I could reach the door, it opened and Aunt Bernadette came in. She looked at us and her face went furtive with shock.

'Sacred Heart,' she whispered, 'Ena.'

Then Uncle Phonsie appeared behind her.

'What is it?'

Ena was lying back on her bed, her eyes stuck open, her hands scrabbling at the coverlet. She started to gasp again, then coughed sharply. It sounded like a fox barking. This time, I moved from the bedside towards the wall, brushing at my shirt. There was a sudden rush of noise, as though someone had turned on a radio. Bernadette was crying as she washed her sister's mouth and face, squeezing the face-cloth into the reddened water that shone in its white enamel basin on the floor. Phonsie disappeared. Then, almost immediately it seemed, the stairs rumbled with running feet and shouts. A doctor came, his stethoscope dangling; then a priest, unscrolling a purple stole.

'Go home and tell your father to come down here this minute. Quick as you can.' They all spoke at once, urging me out.

I went down the stairs three at a time and out into the street where a stiff wind blew, full of the wild smells of the river and the sweetness of the nearby bakery. In the flat light of the evening, everything seemed pale. A man laboured uphill on a bicycle, standing on the pedals, his clothes creasing up at the back and then smoothing out with the effort. I could hear his breath drowning in his throat and then coming free again as I ran past him and took a short cut through the side-streets to the back field. The yard gate was bolted, so I hopped over the wall and jumped clear of the rose-bed below. As I landed my father came out of the shed.

'Ena,' I said, 'Ena's sick. They sent me to tell you.'

He came close and bent down to me. The wind tugged at my hair and rattled the shed door behind him.

'Look at you, child,' he said, 'Look at you. You've got her blood all over you.'

His huge hand touched my cheek. My mother appeared, knowing something was wrong, and came hurrying down the yard.

'Look at him, Mother. Look at him. That's Ena's blood on his shirt; they sent him up like that. Christ, she's taken bad again. She must be . . . '

And he ran after his voice into the house to fetch his jacket and was gone.

At Ena's funeral, after the grave had been closed, Liam motioned me to get in close behind some of the men who were standing around in knots, talking. We would listen and then move away, choking with laughter at their accents and their repetitions. For it wasn't talking; it was more like chanting.

'Man dear, but that's a sore heart this time o' year, wi' Christmas on top o' us and all.'

'It is that, a sore heart indeed.'

'Aye, and at Christmas too.'

'Och ay, so it is. Sore surely.'

They would tug their caps forward by the peak and nod their heads in unison, shuffling their feet slowly.

'Did ye see Bernadette, now; the younger sister?'

'Was that Bernadette? She's far changed now.'

'Far changed indeed. But sure she'd be shook badly now by that death.'

'Aye, the manner o' it. So quick.'

'Still, you can see the likeness to the brother. The dead spit o' him.'

'Which brother d'ye mean?'

'The lost one. Eddie. The wan that disappeared.'

'I never saw him. Is that who she's like? Isn't it strange now, the way families . . . '

Liam and I had stopped laughing. We both listened, but they said little before my father appeared. He motioned us over to him.

'Now there's a double sore heart,' said one of them as we moved off. 'The oldest boy gone, God knows where, and now the youngest sister. Never had good health, God help her.'

He took us to his parents' grave, where we knelt and prayed. *23 December, 1921* for his father. *28 December 1921* for his mother. Their names were blurred on the weathered stone. The graveyard was almost empty when we stood up. Below, the curve of the river disappeared into a high incoming fog that was swelling out of the north Atlantic. My father said nothing, but his mouth looked congested.

So Eddie looked like Bernadette. That was something. But Bernadette, to my eyes, looked like my father. 'Stamped from the same die, what do you expect?' my mother said. Had she ever seen Eddie? As I asked I wondered that I hadn't thought to put this obvious question before. Hardly at all, was her short answer. But that means you did, I persisted, so was he like my father? Very like? Somewhat. She was stalling so I switched. Tell me about the feud. Had Eddie anything to do with that? Child, she'd tell me, I think sometimes you're possessed. Can't you just let the past be the past? But it wasn't the past and she knew it.

So broken was my father's family that it felt to me like a catastrophe you could live with only if you kept it quiet, let it die down of its own accord like a dangerous fire. Eddie gone. Parents both dead within a week. Two sisters, Ena and Bernadette, treated like skivvies and boarded in a hen-house. A long, silent feud. A lost farmhouse, with rafters and books in it, near the field of the disappeared. Silence everywhere. My father knowing something about Eddie, not saying it, not talking but sometimes nearly talking, signalling. I felt we lived in an empty space with a long cry from him ramifying through it. At other times, it appeared to be as cunning and articulate as a labyrinth, closely designed, with someone sobbing at the heart of it.

THE FEUD

February 1950

The feud, the feud. I dreamed of the farmhouse, sunlit and wide, pungent and clean, and of the shy shore-cattle straying on the sand far below, nimble and heavy, the seaweed glittering wet on the shore and drying into mulch on the fields, its foul beach odour dried out to a bitterness in the air.

All the sounds of all the seasons entombed that imagined farmhouse, the white road curled endlessly around it, the skies paused day by day, season by season, in its windows and yet it remained empty, no voice or footfall imaginable within it, except the remembered thunder of my father's feet across a wooden floor and the sensation of being lifted into the air past the slashed light of a window. There must be a cold-water tap outside in the farmyard, I told myself, a manure heap quivering with insects and inner heat, a fox gliding in the dark towards the hen-house with the wind lifting his smell behind him in a soft plume. The suite of imagined odours ran with the screening images, like the background music in a film, and then both would fade and leave me in the still air of the bedroom where I lay with an open book over my face and a sense of frustration marauding in my head.

My father sang as he washed the dishes and scoured the saucepans.

> *Where Lagan stream sings lullaby*
> *There blows a lily fair,*
> *The twilight gleam is in her eye,*
> *The night is on her hair.*

That was a Donegal song, he told me. An old man from

44

Termon used to sing it and his grandfather's father heard it, way in the days before the Famine. It wasn't the River Lagan, the one that flowed through Belfast, just a stream that ran all over the place before it fed into a tributary of the River Foyle. How did he hear it, I wanted to know. Was Great-grandfather a song collector? No, no, the old man who sang it was a roadworker. One day, he gave Great-grandfather directions to the mountain road that ran towards the Poisoned Glen, way out in West Donegal, near Gweedore, and Great-grandfather bought him a pint in a nearby public house. It was there that the old man stood up, took off his cap and sang the song. What did Great-grandfather do? He was a buyer for a grocery firm in Derry. He made contracts with farmers for dairy produce, vegetables, that sort of thing. But the Famine ruined all that. And then the Great War ruined everything later again, for your father, isn't that so? I asked, bending under the sink for a drying cloth and hearing my voice boom a little in the space where the U-pipe took the water into the drain in the back yard. He must have nodded and then he hummed again. This time I sang the second verse to his humming.

> But like a love-sick leannán-sidhe,
> She has my heart in thrall,
> No life I own nor liberty
> For love is lord of all.

I couldn't reach the high notes, and all the grace notes had gone a-quavering, but he smiled anyway and tousled my hair, then laughed when he realised his hands were still soapy and wet. I rubbed my hair with a towel, my eyes blinking a little from a soap bubble that had burst on my eyebrow. 'Good song, that one,' he said. I nodded and said I would love to go into Donegal more often, to that place where Great-grandfather – no my great-great grandfather – had heard it, that place called Termon; or even where Grand-father's family lived, up there in the hills near the Gap of

Mamore, further up the Inishowen peninsula. Some time I would go there, he promised me. Some day he'd take me. To the farmhouse, the one with the rafters? I could still remember the day we were there. It'd be great to see it again. I knew then he was going to tell me something terrible some day, and, in sudden fright, didn't want him to; keep your secrets, I said to him inside my closed mouth, keep your secrets, and I won't mind. But, at the same time, I wanted to know everything. That way I could love him more; but I'd love myself less for making him tell me, for asking him to give me a secret, for having sung a verse of his song, for the accident of having been the one with the flecks of his dead and maltreated sister's blood on him.

Before his parents died, he told me, they used to sing that and other songs together. Eddie was the sweetest singer. I had known he would be. When his parents became ill, they were taken away immediately to the Fever Hospital in the Waterside, across the Foyle, on the other side of the Craigavon Bridge, and he never saw them again, not even at the wake, for the coffins were closed. When the funerals were over, he remembered coming back to the house and finding a lot of the furniture gone already. All the bedlinen was burnt. The house was fumigated and then closed up and the children were all divided between relatives. That's when his sisters went to live with their mother's sister and her husband, in the feud farmhouse in Donegal. It was then, too, that Eddie went away, without warning. My father never saw him again, although he was told Eddie had enlisted down south in the IRA. He couldn't remember how he was told. All he remembered was that the whole world he had known was swept away in a week, in two weeks. He was a child one moment; the next, he was in charge of a whole distraught family of children. He was only twelve, and Eddie, five years older, had gone. He was now the eldest member of the family. He got a job as messenger boy in a hardware store, owned and managed by a Protestant, Mr Edmiston, who sacked him after he had asked for his first raise in five years. It was after that he started to box for a living; later still, he got the job he still had, as a labourer working to an electrician, in the naval base. The children were scattered to the four winds, he said, and at the mercy of anyone and everyone. Uncle Phonsie and my father stayed with cousins, and he remembered his aunt putting out her hand at table to stop Phonsie reaching for the butter. 'You eat margarine,' she told him, 'butter's for the children of this house only.' They left that night, he said, his face reddening slightly even at the memory, stayed in a hostel, and within a week he had rented a room in the Carlisle Road for himself and arranged for Phonsie to go to live with other relatives who promised to treat him as one of their own. And they did. He stayed in that room for four years, living on porridge, potatoes and buttermilk, working, training, starting to box in the ring. Everything in the family home disappeared into the houses of relatives, even down to the photographs. At the time, they were told everything had to be burnt; but that was true only of linens, sheets, towels, that sort of thing. Later, they were told it was the least they could have done, to hand those things over to help pay for their keep. The house was sold. The children never saw a penny of the money. When he visited that farmhouse, he found the place was full of books, furniture, pictures from his parents' home, and his sisters, Ena and Bernadette, were sleeping in pallet beds in a shack beside the hen-house. That's why he'd never even wanted to see those people again. And he never wanted us to have anything to do with them either. And in the meantime, Eddie was fighting for freedom. He shook his head bitterly at that. Freedom. In this place. Never was, never would be. What was it, anyway? Freedom to do what you liked, that was one thing. Freedom to do what you should, that was another. Close enough to one another and far apart as well.

I looked at his bowed head and his large hands, pink-clean from the soapsuds. I wanted to ask him about Eddie to see if he'd tell me, but I didn't want him to tell me only because I asked. He looked up at me, smiling, to say: ah well, it was all blood under the bridge now and I should bother no more with it. I hesitated, then told him I was going out to see if anyone was sailing a kite out in the back field, for the wind was up and it was still bright. But there was no one there, so I spent the evening shooting needle-pointed arrows into the back gate with a bow made from a young tree branch; retrieving them, shooting them, obscurely satisfied only when the arrow struck the wood with a thud and stayed there quivering in a brief and tiny song.

THE FORT

June 1950

Lying in the filtered green light of the high fern-stalks that shook slightly above our heads, we listened to the sharp birdsong of the hillside. This was border country. Less than a mile beyond, a stream, crossed by a hump-backed bridge, marked part of the red line that wriggled around the city on the map and hemmed it in to the waters of Lough Foyle. Every so often, we would stand up clear of the ferns and survey the heathered hills, the pale white roads winding between high hedgerows. Even when no one could be seen, we felt we were watched. When we went down to the bridge, we liked to cross and re-cross it, half-expecting that something punitive would happen because of these repeated violations.

At one end, just above the stream, there was a clump of thorn bushes where wrens turned and twisted endlessly, hooking and unhooking their tiny bodies between the close branches in dapper knitting motions. At the other end, the Free State began – a grassy road that ran straight for thirty yards and then swerved away under an oak tree into that territory where there was an isolated shop, a tin hut thrown up to exploit the post-war food shortages on our side of the border. There the cigarette packets were different, Sweet Afton Virginia in yellow and white with a medallion of Robbie Burns and two lines of the song 'Sweet Afton' slanted underneath across a picture of a stream, a tree, a miniature landscape. The voices of the people there seemed to us as sleek and soft as the glistening wheels of butter on the counter that had a print of a swan on their bright yellow faces. My parents' people came from out there, in Donegal.

One afternoon, Liam and I fell asleep in the warmth of

the fens and woke to a cold evening mist. We decided to go up to the old fort of Grianan, at the top of the hill. Its name meant the Fort of Light, the Sun Fort, we were told, and it had been there for a thousand years. Once at the top, we meant to go downhill on the other, shorter side by a gravel path that connected the fort to the main road below. As we climbed, the mist thickened, and the fort disappeared. We kept close together, sinking now and then into the great spongy pads of fungus that breathed lightly between the stretches of rock and thick-rooted heather. We felt smaller and smaller as the mist rose over us, swarming upward, speeding away past us, yet always arriving again at our feet, in front of our faces, before we could glimpse the lie of the ground beyond. When we thought we could hear the drone of the distant lough, we believed we were nearly there; but the sound would fade and then come again from a different direction, louder, fainter, closer, further away. Only the sudden swoop of bats feeding in mid-air told us for sure that we were near the fort. We knew they favoured the marshy land on its western side. We had often watched them come up the border stream at dusk, hurtling between the trees and then inflecting downward into the clouds of midges that vibrated on the surface. They tracked uphill, over the marshes, as night fell, and we would lose them until they arrived above the fort, squeaking minutely in their blind, curving flight. At the top, we looked into the gathering darkness that welled up towards the Donegal mountains beyond, where the horizon light still survived among streaked clouds. That was where we came from, out of that profile of mountain and darkness where cottage lights twinkled, as distant as stars. Out there were scores of my mother's relatives, all talkative, and just a few of my father's, all silent, all unmet, all locked away in some farm with books and rafters and the feud.

The feud. Did it really start in that farmhouse at Cockhill outside Buncrana — the one with the raftered ceiling and the walls lined with books? Was it really from the wooden floor of that farmhouse that my father swept up my brother and me, followed by my mother, into years of silence? Was it really because he had found out that his sisters were not really living in the house, but were being treated by the family as skivvies and had to sleep in an outhouse, beside the chickens? I remember the great rafters as I rose up in his arms, and the dusty road outside when he put me down, and their voices above us, and the sky above them filling with a great hammerhead cloud off the Atlantic. We never saw the farmhouse again. My father's mother, long dead, came to our house soon afterwards, so my mother told me, and stood at the bottom of the bed as my father slept, watching him, and smiled at my mother, and touched the blankets that covered him and was gone. My mother had a touch of the other world about her. So people would say. And she seemed pleased enough to hear it.

Was that appearance at the foot of the bed a signal from my father's mother that she was pleased with him for having rescued her children and brought them out of their bondage? My mother thought so. I did too. But then I remembered Eddie again. He had not been rescued. But he had nothing to do with the feud, had he? No. He had left soon after his parents died. And when he reappeared, it was only to disappear again in that rosy glow of exploding whiskey.

That was long before the feud, as my mother called it. The feud. The word had a grandeur about it that I savoured, although it occurred to me that maybe there was more to be told. But it was only a half-sense that warned me what I had already been told was not all there was to tell. When I lay on my bed and looked at the picture of the Sacred Heart on the bedroom wall, I thought of Ena's sad eyes as she fell back dying on the bed; its eyes watched me, whether I moved or lay still. Its mournfulness always gave me the same sensation that there was a deeper sorrow in the family than I could yet know, that the eyes were asking me to acknowledge the sharpness of a grief that could so pierce the heart.

51

FIELD OF THE DISAPPEARED

August 1950

In the summer of 1950 we had more money because my father was working overtime in the dockyards. We could, therefore, afford a holiday – two weeks in a boarding-house in Buncrana. My father came down on the bus at the weekends, for he could not get the time off during the week. The weather was hot, unbroken, bright as metal. When we wearied of the lough shore, we walked in the hills beyond the town, escorting ourselves carefully away from Cockhill and the feud-farm, as we called it, where my father's people seemed to us to hide, recessed into the hills. But on the first Sunday he came down, my father took Liam and me for a walk out the road that climbed steadily, curve by curve, towards the very place, nearer and nearer to where we believed the farm was. We glanced at one another, but said nothing. Instead, we looked blindly at the shivery furrows the wind opened in the hissing corn, at the potato drills stretching across the gently steepening slopes, and at the gulls drifting lazily inland before they banked towards the cliffs on the coast. He wanted to show us something, he said. His forehead glistened; his reddish hair was receding, making his craggy face more exposed, kinder, sweeter. He was walking heavily, not with his usual jaunt. Liam looked so like him that day: the same colouring, the same sharpness in his blue eyes. I was dark, like my mother, and felt almost like a member of another family beside them.

We came round a bend in the road that swept us out towards the ocean and then began to wrinkle inland again in a series of shallow loops. We stopped on the outer rim of the road. He pointed towards the sea.

'Can you see anything peculiar?' he asked.

We looked. Fields ran down to the cliff edge, lifting in a wave before they reached it. We saw nothing odd. We climbed a gate and went downfield into a shallow dell, thick with clover, buttercups, dandelions, daisies; it curved up and yielded to the final fold of ground that jutted into air as a lip of the cliff. From there, when we looked up, the grass seemed to stretch out into mid-air, yards beyond the rockier ground on either side. That stretch of green, he told us, was what we were to watch. We should be patient; look at the birds. They would fly towards it but were never really above it. We watched. Gulls, starlings, a swallow, all hung or soared in the air. They were so high it was hard to tell if they were above the patch or not; but certainly none landed on it, although some came near. Why? What was it? Tell us, we asked. That, he said, is the Field of the Disappeared. The birds that came toward it would pass from view and then come back on either side; but if they flew across it, they disappeared. We watched. My heart was thudding, even though I thought he was joking at first. The sea heaved in my ears and boomed far below, over and over. No, it was the truth, he said. That was its name. The local farmers avoided it. There was a belief that it was here that the souls of all those from the area who had disappeared, or had never had a Christian burial, like fishermen who had drowned and whose bodies had never been recovered, collected three or four times a year – on St Brigid's Day, on the festival of Samhain, on Christmas Day – to cry like birds and look down on the fields where they had been born. Any human who entered the field would suffer the same fate; and any who heard their cries on those days should cross themselves and pray out loud to drown out the sound. You weren't supposed to hear pain like that; just pray you would never suffer it. Or if you were in a house when the cries came, you were meant to close the doors and windows to shut them out, in case that pain entered your house and destroyed all in it. Christmas was a silent day in that valley, he said, especially when the evening came. I looked up at him and into his eyes. He smiled a little at me, but his face was troubled. Again, I felt there was something more to be told, but his eyes were saying he had changed his mind, he was not going to say any more.

We stared for a while longer at the grass on that patch wavering in a mirage of wind, although the day was still. I wondered what it was like in those days of February, November and December when the cries came. I went a little further up the slope to get closer to the magic field.

'Don't,' said my father, 'that's far enough.'

I stopped. I wanted to go on. I looked back at him, standing there, waiting, his eyes squeezed against the sunlight. Liam stood between us. A gull landed on a nearby rock. I wanted to go on towards the cliff edge. I took another couple of steps upward. The slope was steeper than it looked. My father said nothing. Liam went back towards him and sat down among the buttercups. Is this, I wondered, where Eddie's soul comes to cry for his lost fields? Dare I ask? I didn't. Nor did I want to go closer to the edge. So I came downhill again to ask him if he had ever heard the cries. No. Had he ever wanted to hear them? No. If you could recognise the cry of someone lost to you amid the others? He didn't know, didn't think so. By this time he was walking back towards the gate. When did he first hear about this field? He couldn't remember. I felt angry. He was blocking me, he had brought us here and then he walked away, with no explanation.

'I don't believe all that,' I told him, 'I think it's all made up.'

'No doubt,' he answered drily.

'I mean, who'd believe that? Birds disappearing. Look, there's one, that gull, right above it.'

I pointed but the gull was wheeling away, its cry scrawling the path of its flight.

Back on the road, we looked towards the field again. Now it looked quite ordinary. We could see the cliff edge where it ended. Then, as the sunlight flashed off the sea, for

54

a moment, I could have sworn I saw someone standing there, right at the edge, a man peering down at the waters folding softly below. But when I looked again, there was no one. I came off the high camber and half-ran to the other side of the road, where Liam was cutting a switch from a bush with his penknife, hacking it angrily. My father was ahead of us, walking quite fast. I reached to help hold the switch stick straight while Liam sliced off the side twigs. He looked at me furiously.

'Get lost, you. Go up there and walk with him.'

And I ran to catch up with him but, as in a dream, he seemed never to get nearer and I gave up, stranded between them, Liam at the hedge paring his switch and looking at me, my father's back receding as he came to a turn in the road, the gulls' cries ringing piteously, angrily, in my ears.

GRIANAN

September 1950

Grianan was a great stone ring with flights of worn steps on the inside leading to a parapet that overlooked the countryside in one direction and the coastal sands of the lough in the other. At the base of one inside wall, there was a secret passage, tight and black as you crawled in and then briefly higher at the end where there was a wishing-chair of slabbed stone. You sat there and closed your eyes and wished for what you wanted most, while you listened for the breathing of the sleeping warriors of the legendary Fianna who lay below. They were waiting there for the person who would make that one wish that would rouse them from their thousand-year sleep to make final war on the English and drive them from our shores forever. That would be a special person, maybe with fairy eyes, a green one and a brown one, I thought, or maybe a person with an intent in him, hard and secret as a gun in his pocket, moving only when he could make everything else move with him. I was terrified that I might, by accident, make that special wish and feel the ground buckle under me and see the dead faces rise, indistinct behind their definite axes and spears.

Liam and I spent a large part of our school holidays there in the summer. When there were others with us, we would break into groups and have races to the fort at the top. The winners then defended the fort against the rest, struggling wildly on the parapet, scaling the walls, our cries lost in the wild heather and rocks of the reserved landscape.

Once, my friends – Moran, Harkin, Toland – locked me in the secret passage. At first, I hardly reacted at all – just sat there in the stone wishing-chair. Gradually, the dark passageway up which I had just crawled lost its vague roundness and simply became blackness. I sat there, cold, even though it was hot outside and there were larks lost in song on high warm thermals above the old fort. I touched the wet walls and felt the skin of slime sliding in slow motion over their hardness. Even there, it stirred something in me to move my hand up against the wrinkling moss and water. If I were out and on the circular parapet again, I would see Inch Island and the wide flat estuaries of the dark-soiled coast and hear the distant war noise of the sea grumbling beyond. But here, inside the thick-walled secret passage which ended in this chair-shaped niche, there was nothing but the groan of the light breeze in that bronchial space, and the sound of water slitting into rivulets on the sharp rock face. I imagined I could hear the breathing of the sleeping Fianna waiting for the trumpet call that would bring them to life again to fight the last battle which, as the prophecies of St Columcille told us, would take place somewhere between Derry and Strabane, after which the one remaining English ship would sail out of Lough Foyle and away from Ireland forever. If you concentrated even further, you would scent the herbal perfumes of the Druid spells and you would hear the women sighing in sexual pleasure – yes–esss–yes–esss. If you then made a wish, especially a love-wish, you would always be attractive to women.

My friends had done this. I had been sitting there, in the wishing-chair, wondering how I could concentrate more on the emaciated ghost sounds within the passage, when the little light there was disappeared. I heard the grunt of the stone that covered the entrance being rolled back into place to shut me in. I yelled, but they laughed and ran up the parapet steps above me. The stone could not be moved from inside the passageway; it was too narrow to allow for leverage. So I sat and waited. When I shouted, my voice ricocheted all around me and then vanished. I had never known such blackness. I could hear the wind, or maybe it was the far-off sea. That was the breathing Fianna. I could smell the heather and the gorse tinting the air; that was the

Druid spells. I could hear the underground waters whispering; that was the women sighing. The cold was marrow-deep; the chair seemed to shine with it. A scuttling, as of field mice, would come and go; perhaps it was mortar trickling away from the stones. I crawled down to the entrance and shouted again. Eventually, someone came and rolled the stone back and I scrambled out into the sunshine, dazed by the light, unsteady when I walked, as though all my blood had collected around my ankles. Later, when we climbed to the parapet again and scrambled down the wall to the road that took us home, the sky and the hills around seemed so wide and high that the dark passageway felt even worse in retrospect, more chilling and enclosed.

We had crossed the border by more than a field's width and were approaching the road when a car came round a bend and almost caught us in its lights. We ducked into the darkness of the hedgerow. 'Water rats,' said Brendan Moran, peering up after them. It was the nickname given to customs officers. 'Looking for smugglers. My father told me the smugglers caught one of them one night near Grianan and they took his customs jacket off, tied him up and closed him inside the passage. It was nearly two days before they found him, and he was stark, staring mad when they got him out. He's still in the asylum at Gransha and they say he's always cold; never warmed up since. Never will.'

As we came over the last rise in the road, the city lay braided in lights below us. We seemed to fall towards it, too tired to talk, into the network of narrow streets on that still Indian summer's night.

KATIE'S STORY

October 1950

So there it was, our territory, with the old fort of Grianan on one hill overlooking Lough Foyle, the feud farmhouse on another hill, gazing on Lough Swilly, the thick neck of the Inishowen peninsula between, Derry gauzed in smoke at the end of Lough Foyle, the border writhing behind it. We would walk out there into Donegal in the late morning and be back in the city by six o'clock, in time to see the women and girls streaming home from the shirt factories, arms linked, so much more brightly dressed, so much more talkative than the men, most of whom stood at the street corners. We would call to them, but they would dismiss us as youngsters.

'Wheel that fella home in his pram. His mother'll be lookin' for him.'

'You and your wee red cheeks. Teethin' again!'

We'd retreat in disarray. Sometimes, the older boys would jump on to the back of a lorry or hang on to the luggage ladder on a bus and fly past them, whistling, shouting the names of girls and the boys who fancied them. When the women disappeared into the houses there was always a blank space, a stillness of air disrobed, gaiety lost. Smoke from the chimneys stood up in the sky, even in summer, and when one went on fire, the sheaf of flame was a delight to see.

Katie, my mother's sister, had been working in Tilly and Henderson's factory as a stitcher. She had married young, way before my mother. Her one child, a daughter, Maeve, was already in her twenties and worked in a newsagent's. Her husband, Maeve's father, had disappeared even before Maeve was born, when Katie was only a couple of months pregnant. It wasn't much talked about. His name was Tony

McIlhenny. He had gone out to America in 1926, it seemed, looking for work, wrote once or twice, then nothing. He had left very suddenly; rumour had it that he had gone to Chicago, that he was married there and had children and was a respected member of his community. But he had never seen his child, never contacted her. It was strange. Katie never spoke of him. Once, when Liam asked my mother about him, she shook him by the shoulder and told him never to mention that man's name in the house again. 'Jesus,' said Liam, 'ask and ye shall receive. Jesus.'

In a way, Katie adopted us and became a second mother. I used to wish she would stay in with us more and that my parents would go out to the movies together. But they never did. They went nowhere together — not that there were many places to go, except to other people's houses for a chat and a ceilidh, as they called it. Had they ever gone out together? I asked Eilis and Liam because they were older, but they didn't remember them ever going out. Anyway, what was strange about it? They lived in one another's pocket. That's what married people do, Eilis said. Yes. But still, I wished they would go out together. 'Costs money,' said Liam. 'And there isn't any. Simple.'

Because Katie had no children to look after, now that Maeve was grown up, she was freer to go out than anyone else; besides, she was out of work. The shirt factory at the end of Craigavon Bridge had laid off scores of women when work got scarce. She didn't think she would work again. So she came up to our house more often now and sometimes let my mother go upstairs for a nap while she looked after things in the kitchen. I watched the different ways she did things. She used more coal and kept the fire brighter; she put the saucepans on the range with their handles turned to the left rather than to the right. She sat with her back to the window. My mother always sat facing it. 'There now,' she would say, when she finished doing something. 'There now.' She could never get the amounts straight when she was giving me the order for the grocer's.

60

'God bless us, you don't need four loaves. One will do.'

'You're used to buying for just two people, Katie. There's eight in this house.'

'Yes,' she said, 'never more than two. You're right.'

She had always told us bedtime stories when we were younger, with good and bad fairies; or mothers whose children had been taken by the fairies but were always restored; haunted houses; men who escaped from danger and got back to their families; stolen gold; unhappy rich people and their lonely children; houses becoming safe and secure after overcoming threats from evicting landlords and police; saints burned alive who felt no pain; devils smooth and sophisticated who always wore fine clothes and talked in la-de-dah ways. She had so many accents and so many voices that it hardly mattered to us if we got mixed up in the always labyrinthine plot. Now that we were growing up, all that had stopped. But she would still tell stories of a different kind, downstairs in the kitchen, if we got her in the mood and if my parents were not there. I always felt their presence as a kind of censorship on what Katie would say.

'There was this young woman called Brigid McLaughlin,' she told Eilis and me one afternoon, after we had helped her with a big laundering of clothes and were all sitting about the kitchen, Katie in the armchair with her back to the window and her feet up on a pile of cushions. My mother was asleep upstairs. 'Mind you, this was long before my time. I heard it from your Great-uncle Constantine's mother, God be good to them both.' She fell to brooding for a while. We didn't stir. This was her way of telling a story. If you hurried her up, she cut it short and it lost all its wonder.

Brigid had been hired – no, not at one of the hiring fairs in the city centre, where young men and women gathered to be hired out for the winter to work in the hinterland farms – hired by a private arrangement to look after two children, two orphans, a boy and a girl, who lived away down in the southern part of Donegal where they still spoke Irish, but an Irish that was so old that many other Irish speakers couldn't follow it. Brigid had been brought up there before coming up here to Derry, so the language was no problem to her. Anyway, these children's uncle was going away to foreign parts and he wanted someone to look after them and educate them a bit. Now one of the odd things about these children was their names. The boy was called Francis, and the girl was called Frances. Even in Irish you couldn't tell the names apart, except in writing. No one knows why their parents christened them so. The parents themselves, they had been carried off by the cholera during the Great Famine, though they were well enough off themselves and had never starved. Anyway, however it was, this young woman – Brigid – was sent down there to look after them. She had a year's contract, signed in her father's house. But she was not, for all of that year, to leave the children out of her charge and was never to take them away from the house itself. Everything she needed would be supplied, on the uncle's arrangement, by the shopkeepers in the village a couple of miles away. So off she went to this big farmhouse in the middle of nowhere to look after Frances, the girl, who was nine, and Francis, the boy, who was seven.

She wrote home to her father for the first few months and all seemed to be well. But then the letters stopped altogether. It was only after it was over that people found out what had happened.

The children were beautiful, especially the girl. She was dark, the boy was fair. They spoke Irish only. Brigid taught them all she knew, every morning for two hours, every afternoon for one hour. But they had this habit, they told Brigid, that they had promised each other never to break. Every day they would go to the field behind the house, where their parents were buried, and put flowers on the grave and sit there for a long time. They always asked her to leave them alone to do this; she could watch them, they said, from an upstairs window. So Brigid did that. And all was well. But, after some time had passed, and summer had waned, Brigid tried to discourage them more strongly, for it was often wet and beginning to get cold. Still, the children insisted. On one particularly bad day in the autumn, when the rain was coming down in sheets, and the wind was howling, she stopped them going. She wouldn't give in. And they, in turn, insisted. Finally, she put them in their rooms and told them that was the end of it. They could visit their parents' grave in decent weather, but she wasn't going to have them falling ill by doing so in such conditions, no more than their parents would want her to, or want them to insist on doing. After a big quarrel, the first they ever had, the children went to their rooms and, after a bit, when it was dark, Brigid went to bed. Now, would you believe this? It's the God's truth. The next morning, when she went to their rooms, what did she find? She found the boy was now dark-haired, as his sister had been, and the girl was fair-haired, as her brother had been. And they didn't seem to notice! They told her they had always been like this, that she was imagining things. You can imagine! Poor Brigid! She thought she was going out of her mind. She examined them all over; she questioned them; she threatened not to give them any meals until they told her the truth. But they just sat there, telling her she was the one who had got everything wrong. Right, says Brigid, we'll see who's imagining things. We'll go into the village. We'll go to the priest. We'll go to anyone we meet and we'll put the question to them. The children agreed, and off they went to the parochial house and found the priest in and waited in the drawing room to meet him. Brigid sat down and then got up and sat down again while the children, polite and well-mannered as they usually were, sat before her on straight-backed chairs, quiet and as assured as any two grown-ups would have been. When the priest came in, Brigid went straight to him and said, 'Father, Father, for the love of God, look at these two children, Francis and Frances, and tell me what has happened, for I don't know if they're in the hands of the devil or what.' And the priest, very surprised and shocked, looked at her, looked at them, caught her by the wrist and sat her down, shaking his head and asking her what did she mean; to take it slowly, tell him again. But the children, she cried at him, look at the children, they've changed, they've switched colours. Look! She pointed at them and there they were, looking at her and the priest, and they were the colour and complexion they had always been, the girl dark, and the boy fair. We told her, they said to the priest, we have always been like this but she says we changed colour and she frightened us. Both of them began to cry, and Brigid began to wail and the priest ran between them like a scalded cat for a while before he could calm things down.

Poor Brigid! She knew the priest thought she was going strange, the children were so loud in their protests and so genuinely upset that she began to wonder herself. Especially as the children kept their complexions just as they had been for days and days after, and during those days, no matter what the weather, Brigid let them visit their parents' grave and watched them from the upstairs window and saw nothing wrong. But she couldn't sleep at night, for she knew, she knew, she knew that she had not been mistaken. She could clearly remember examining them – running her hands up the back of their hair, seeing the boy's skin that shade darker, the girl's skin that white and pink that had been the boy's. She knew she had not imagined this, and yet there it was! She lay in the bed clutching her rosary beads and saying her prayers and every so often shaking with a fit of the weeps, for she knew either she was mad, or there was something very strange in that house and very frightening about those children. With all this sleeplessness, she took to walking about her room and now and again she would pull back the curtain to look outside. Over to the left was the field where the grave lay. It was no more than a week after she had gone to the priest that she looked out one night and saw to her terror that there was a kind of greenish light shimmering above the grave, and in that light she could see the children standing there, hand-in-hand, staring down at the ground

64

where the light seemed to be welling up. She was so terrified that when she tried to cry out she could not; when she wanted to move, she was paralysed; when she wanted to cry, her eyes were dry-dead in her head. She didn't know how long she stood like that but eventually she moved and forced herself out the door and as she did she began to wail their names – Francis, Frances, Frances, Francis – over and over as she rushed along the corridor. With that, she heard them, in their bedrooms, crying out and went to find them wakened and terrified, still warm and dry, both of them, still with sleep in their eyes. She brought them to her room and put them in her bed, shook holy water over them, told them to pray, told them not to be frightened, made herself go to the window again and look and all was dark – no greenish light, no figures of children at the grave. The night passed somehow. The children slept. She lay in the bed alongside them and held them as close as she dared without waking them. But when they woke and asked her for breakfast and what had happened, she went cold all over. For now their voices were changed. The boy had the girl's voice, and the girl had the boy's voice. She put her hands over her ears. She shut her eyes. Then she said she became calm for a moment. She knew she had to see. So she asked the children to come with her to the bathroom to wash before they ate. She helped them undress, even though they usually undressed themselves. And sure enough, their sex had changed too. The boy was a girl, and the girl was a boy. And they paid no notice! They washed themselves and said nothing. She made them breakfast; she gave them lessons, she let them out to play under the apple trees in the front garden. She knew, she said, that if she brought them to the priest or the doctor, the same thing would happen: they would change back and leave her looking like a lunatic. She knew, too, that if she left the house – even if she could find a way of doing so, for there was little or no transport to be had and certainly none to take them as far north as Derry – and there was nowhere else she could think of – something terrible would happen. She knew now she was being challenged by evil, and the children were being stolen from her by whatever was in that grave out the back. Oh, she knew without knowing how she knew it. There was no question.

Katie paused for a long time. The clock on the mantelpiece ticked. Eilis was bending down in her chair, her hair falling over her face. I wanted to peep in the shaving mirror on the wall to make sure my hair was still dark. Katie went on brooding. A coal in the fire cracked and little blue flames began to hiss. There was no sound from upstairs. Some families, Katie told us, are devil-haunted. You see that young girl, Brigid McLaughlin? She was the same family as poor Larry up yonder on the street corner, him that never talks now, since he saw the devil on the day before his marriage. You remember that story? Eilis did. She nodded her head. I didn't. But I wanted Katie to go on with this story, so I nodded too. She went on. It's a curse a family can never shake off. Maybe it's something terrible in the family history, some terrible deed that was done in the past, and it just spreads and it spreads down the generations like a shout down that tunnel, the secret passage, in the walls of Grianan, that echoes and echoes and never really stops. It's held in those walls forever.

An instinct woke in me at the mention of Grianan. I wanted her to stop, not knowing why, but she went on. I wished my mother would come awake, or that someone would come in and interrupt Katie. But everyone seemed to have gone. In an hour, the factory girls would be coming out, the place would be alive with people, Katie would rush to get the dinner ready, I would scrub down the deal table, Eilis would start clattering the knives and forks. Deirdre, Liam, Gerard and Eamon would all come in, my father would arrive, my mother would appear, people would be chattering about this and that, the radio would be turned on for the news.

Anyway, anyway, Katie continued, passing her hand over her broad, kind face in a circular, washing movement, there the poor girl was, locked in with something terrible and the two strange children changing over from one to another before her very eyes. She wrote down in a notebook all the changes there were: changes from boy to girl, changes back to what they had been when she first came. Some of the changes were smaller than others. One day, it would be the colour of their eyes. The girl's would be blue, although she was still dark-haired and olivy-skinned; the boy's would be brown. Another day, it would be their height. The girl was a little taller, normally, but one day she was the boy's height, and he hers. One day, she swore, it was their teeth changed. She had his smile, and he had hers. Another day, it was their ears. Another day, their hands. On and on, for thirty-two days she watched these changes. The children continued to sleep in her room, and on seven of the nights throughout those days she saw the greenish light on the grave and the figures of the children standing there, hand-in-hand, even while they were lying asleep in her bed with her. By now, it was deep into November. She was living as if she might explode at any minute but she kept her panic down. When anyone came to visit – the priest, the doctor, a tradesman – the children were always as they should be. No matter how she watched, she never saw the moment of change from one condition to the next. Then, suddenly, everything got worse.

She was brushing Frances's hair in front of a long free-standing mirror that you could adjust to whatever angle you liked. It had a wooden frame, a mix, she said, of two woods: one was called bird's-eye maple and the other rosewood. She wouldn't have known this, but the children told her. They knew every detail of every article of furniture, every piece of china, every item of cutlery, every floor-covering and wall hanging, every picture and clock, in the house. They knew the names of the local people to whom the farmland had been rented out for pasture; they knew the conditions of the rental; they knew the grazing in the different fields – everything! Brigid had just finished brushing the girl's hair and was giving it a final stroke or two when she looked and saw herself in the mirror, standing there with the brush in one hand and the other cupped in mid-air, as though holding something. But the girl wasn't there, wasn't in the mirror, although Brigid was touching her, holding the strands of the child's hair in her hand. She stood there, stock-still, wanting to fall to the ground, keeping herself upright by dint of her will. The boy was in the room at the time and he came over, asking her to hurry up and finish brushing for he wanted to go downstairs and play. He moved into the frame of the mirror and he too disappeared. She asked them to look and they did, and she asked them if they could see themselves, and they said yes, of course they could, and they laughed, but uneasily. And they could see her too, they said. The grandfather clock in the bedroom corridor struck at that moment, struck ten strokes. She remembered that. She counted them. It was ten o'clock in the morning of the twenty-first of November. And that clock never moved a solitary inch thereafter. It stopped and it never started again.

Now she didn't know that then, but that was the very hour and day the parents of those children had died, five years before. They both died at the same time. But she only learned that later. And it was then that the children stopped going out to the grave every day. It was then they stopped the changes. It was then, she said, that she knew the two people in the grave outside had finally come into the house. She went to the priest and asked him to come and bless the house. He did. He walked all through it, bearing the host with him, saying the Latin prayers, throwing the dashes of holy water on all the doors, all the exits and entrances. When he had done, he asked Brigid why she had covered up all the mirrors in the house. She told him. He commanded her then to bring the children to him in front of the big mirror in the bedroom and he took off the velveteen cloth she had draped over it and stood them in front of him before the mirror. And there they were, just as normal. He would have to do something about this, he said; he would write to the uncle and see what could be done. The doctor would call and see her, and his housekeeper would come in now and then to help her. At least January wasn't far off and then she could go back home for the uncle would have returned by then. So, all this was done. But when Brigid was left alone, as she had to be, she felt the presence of the dead parents all over again; the house was colder, and, every so often, she would see the greenish light under the door of one of the rooms that had been closed up or fading away at the end of the upstairs corridor or thinning out to a mossy line in the frame of a window as she entered a room.

Then one night, she said, they came for the children. Francis and Frances were in her bed as usual. They lay there awake, unable to sleep, and the little girl began to sing a song Brigid had never heard before in a language that was not Irish or Latin or English, and the little boy joined in. Brigid stood before them, a crucifix in her hand, praying, praying, with the flesh prickling all over her. Those children lay there, she said, their voices in unison, singing this sad, slow air, and all the changes she had seen before passing over them, one by one, faster and faster, until she didn't know which was the boy, which the girl. The whole house was booming, as with the sound of heavy feet on the wooden stair. The greenish light came into the room in mid-air and spread all over it, and with that came this whispering of voices, a man's and a woman's, whispering, whispering, furious, almost as if they were spitting in anger, except that the voices were dry, whipped up like swirlings of dust in a wind. The children stopped their singing and sat up in their bed, their eyes standing in their heads, their mouths open but without sound, their arms outstretched to Brigid. She opened her arms to them, dropping the crucifix on the bed, and she says she felt them, their hands and their arms, felt her own hands touching their shoulders, and, with that, the greenish light disappeared, the whispering stopped, and the children were gone. All that was left was the warmth of the bed, the dents in the pillows, the wind whistling outside.

She got the priest out of his bed in the middle of that night, and he came with her, hurrying down the road, buttoning his long coat, telling her she should not have left the children, that this was the last straw, she'd have to go home. But when they got to the empty house and searched it and found no children, he began to accuse her of having made off with them and was going to get the doctor, who had a pony and trap, to go to the next town for the police. Oh, Father, she said, do that. Do what you must. But before you do, come out the back with me. She led him to the grave, and there they saw, the both of them, the greenish light wavering over the mound of earth and heard, clear as a lark song, the voices of the two children, coming from the heart of the light, singing, singing their strange air. The priest blessed himself and fell on his knees, as did Brigid with him, and they stayed there in the wind and the rain until morning when the greenish light faded and the voices of the children with it.

The children were never seen again.

All the mirrors in the house had been shattered, all the clocks were stopped at the hour of ten, only the children's clothes were left to show that they had once been there. God knows what the uncle thought when he came back. Brigid was taken home, the uncle came to see her, she talked to him, she talked to everyone who would listen for maybe six months after her return, she went completely strange in the head and people used to bless themselves when she appeared and hurry away. Then Brigid stopped talking. Until the day she died she never spoke again, would never leave her room, would never have a mirror near her. Only every year, on the twenty-first of November, you could hear her up in her room, singing this song, in words none could understand, a song no one had ever heard, that must have been the song the children sang that night long ago, in south

Donegal, only five years after the Famine. And the blight's on that family to this very day.

At last, my mother moved upstairs, the bells of the cathedral began to ring, and the noises of the world outside came dappling in as Katie blessed herself, laughed and shook her head at something, and told me to get the scrubbing-brush and warm water for the table. Eilis sat there, her hair falling fair over her obscured face.

PART TWO

PART TWO

CHAPTER THREE

RATS

November 1950

In the winter of 1947, the snow had covered the air-raid shelters out in the back field. No one ever used the shelters during the war, not even after the bombing of Belfast. When the Americans began to arrive, in their thousands, some people said we were in for it now. But the Germans came once only, made a bombing run on the docks where the American ships were lined up in threes and fours, missed, and never came again. The sirens had given several false alarms before, but this time the throb of the approaching planes seemed to make them more frenetic. We woke to their wild moanings, were carried to safety under the stairs and cradled sleepily between our parents, lightly asperged by the bright drops of cold Lourdes water that my mother would every so often sprinkle on us. I remember the silence when the droning stopped and then the long lamentation of each plane's dive. One or two guns pumped. Then the house seemed to lift a little on a wave of sound. When the all-clear sounded, my father remembered the air-raid shelters, where we should have gone, and laughed.

There were five shelters, built in a line parallel with the street, from the top of the sloping field to the bottom. The last was almost opposite our back gate. Made of red brick and concrete slab roofs, they echoed like empty stone boxes. Our feet rang in them and our voices boomed. They stank of urine and cheap wine, for derelicts used to sit there drinking, sprawled against the wall as though they had been shot, their eyes razor-slit with exhaustion. Once as I ran through them, I saw two tinkers, a man and a woman, wrestling on the floor; I almost ran into their heaving foetor of split clothes and white skin. Vomit was rising up in my throat as I got out again into the field. For ages afterwards, I could envisage them clearly, he butting back and forth on top of her, she writhing slowly, one leg in mid-air. I didn't know what I had seen, but I said nothing.

When the shelters were demolished, in late spring, 1950, the broken rubble was left strewn along the edge of the field out the back. After a time, it began to be used as a dumping ground. Within months, we had a rat problem. The City Corporation did nothing, despite the rats scampering and squeaking. When I went outside to shovel coal from the back shed into the fire-bucket, a rat would streak through the door when I opened it or scarper to the back of the coal pile when I drove the shovel in to its base. Soon, they were appearing in the houses. We would have to destroy them in their nests in the rubble.

The men of the neighbourhood dug deep trenches at each end of the line of rubble, building the excavated earth into a steep slope to make it harder for the emerging rats to escape. Then they half-filled the trenches with anything that would burn – newspapers, oilcloth, shards of linoleum, broken planks. They sprinkled this with pink paraffin. We were deputed to collect all the dogs of the neighbourhood. There were collies, greyhounds, Kerry Blues with their steel-trap jaws, terriers of every description and mongrels that defied any. We patrolled on top of the rubble, hissing at the dogs, slapping them on the jaws and jumping back as they snarled and twisted on their leads. When a dog stopped and sniffed or barked at an exit hole in the rubble, we blocked it with stones or thrust burning, paraffin-soaked rags down on a stick and piled in paper and dried grass on top until there was a smoky mass curling up. Then we blocked it as best we could and watched for exit plumes of smoke at other parts of the rubble. We blocked these too. Soon the whole stretch was drifting with smoke. We wore our gas masks as we moved up and down in lines, looking like creatures with inflated and goggled insect heads, holding the dogs tight on the leashes as they strained and whimpered.

The rats began to emerge, first from the deep trenches at either end. The men stood above with blazing torches in their hands. They waited, as the rats bolted back and forth, leaping every so often, like salmon, to clear the sloping earth bank above. Then, when the trench was packed with the squeaking, twisting creatures, they threw in the torches, the paraffin exploded, and the flames wavered up at each end, simultaneously, then closed their silky curtains in a swift hiss over the length of the trench. Standing on top of the rubble we could hear the rats and feel them moving. Then they began to come out from the bolt holes, some of them muscled, slug-like, others hairy and squalid, all of them darting or scurrying at an amazing speed. We released the dogs and picked up branches, hurling sticks, iron bars or makeshift spears, made of two or three bamboo poles lashed together and sharpened at the end or with a blade fixed on top. The dogs caught the rats in their jaws and tossed them back and forth. Some rats escaped into the darkness behind us, and we sent the greyhounds after them. The dead ones were pitched into the flames; others we forced back with our sticks and spears until, twisting and turning, they slipped over the edge into the blazing trenches, from which they would sometimes leap in mid-air, squealing in agony.

We had begun in late afternoon. By dark, the battle was over. We were poking in the embered trenches, heavy with the massed bodies of the rats, when we heard one of the mongrels bark and then yelp with fear. From the middle of the rubble, a rat was emerging, dazed with smoke. It seemed to come out in sections, as though it were a snake. 'A king rat,' said someone, and we rushed it with the dogs. It screamed like a baby piglet as we came for it and fled from the rubble heap, but we pinned it to the wall of one of the back yards. The dogs turned hesitantly, barking, but not going in. The rat rose on its hind legs, screeching from its red and grey mouth, its whitish belly exposed. Finally we enraged a Kerry Blue, slapping it on the nose, poking it in the flanks until it was snapping round in tight, violent circles.

Then we lifted it and threw it on the rat so that it had to bite or be bitten. The rat's head almost came off with the second snap.

Going home through the smoke-swirls and the noise, the mock-burial parties for the dead rats that were being covered by the clay from the trenches, the poles tipped with knives clashing in skirmishes, I felt so sick that the flesh seemed to tighten on my bones. The infested field was glowing and blurring like an inferno. Even the night sky seemed vague, as the smoke drifted across the starlight, and I imagined the living rats that remained, breathing their vengeance in a dull miasmic unison deep underground.

CRAZY JOE

August 1951

It was Crazy Joe Johnson who got me into the art room of
the public library. Everybody called him Crazy Joe. He was
always walking around the streets, talking to everyone he
met, especially children. He rarely made sense to us, but we
had been told not to make fun of him; something had
happened when he was a young man and he had never been
right since. He had no harm in him; the only harm in Joe
had been done to him by someone else. So we were told; I
wasn't so sure. He made me feel uneasy. He was often in or
around the library, nodding and smiling to himself, humming, twirling his walking stick, raising his hat to women,
real or imagined. He had a sculpted, clean appearance. His
medallion face fronted his large head like a mask, and the
head itself, perched on his tiny body, swung and vibrated all
the time like an insect's. His smile was brilliant for his teeth
were false and his speech was as precise and fumigated as the
rest of him, all lips and teeth and tip of the tongue.

On a summer evening, after playing football up at Rosemount, I came through the public park on my way to the
library to borrow books for the weekend. The librarian, a
formidable Protestant lady, clucked her tongue at me but
let me through the wooden turnstile beside the desk after
inspecting my hands by turning them over like a pair of
dried fish on the blotting paper at the counter. She was large,
her blouse tight on her breasts, her throat slightly goitrous.
In her armour of chiffon and serge, with her blondish hair
rigidly waved, she seemed to pulse softly and secretly. Even
on this occasion, when I was still streaked with sweat from
the football, she pursed her lips in determined disapproval

and then smiled as she let me through. Her friendliness was stronger than her sense of respectability.

Once through, I went straight to the door of the art room. 'Reserved for Adults' declared the black-and-white lettering across the glass door with its mahogany trim and ornate brass and wooden handle. Joe was in there on his own, standing at a lectern, turning an immense page that flashed colour and left a brief rainbow on his hand. On seeing me, he immediately came towards the door in quick, martinet steps. I retreated towards the Young Readers section, grabbed the first book that came to hand and pretended to read. Joe arrived, beaming, took the book from my hand, placed it back on the shelf and whispered,

'Let me show you something.'

He held me by the sleeve and led me towards the room. 'I'm not allowed in there. It's for adults only.'

'Tosh, pure tosh. If I invite you in, no permission is required. Miss Knowles will be only too pleased to see a hot little savage like yourself come under the cool shade of my educative influence. Right, Miss Knowles?'

He raised his voice in her direction, but she seemed not to hear him and kept her eyes on the box of filing cards she was arranging with minute care.

'You see? Idiot boy. Come.'

So we went in. He led me across to the book he had been looking at, wide open on the wooden lectern. The colours were thick and dark. I did not know how to look properly. The shapes jumped from the page and then coiled down again. He shut the book in a handclap of dustbeams.

'I think not. Let us begin with the French. Here we are. Feast your eyes, young fellow, feast your eyes and say nothing, for you can say nothing that will not be ridiculous.'

It was a painting of a naked woman. Her body lay on dark velvet and was both sprawled and private. The colours of her flesh were interfused like fragrances.

'Oh,' I exclaimed.

'O-ho,' Joe chortled, 'young Caliban sees beauty. The

beauty of Boucher, young sir, will stir the sensibilities of even such an outcast as thou art.'

And he slammed the book shut.

'Out with you now. Too much too quickly will disturb the savage breast. Return to your trash. Get thee gone.'

He waved me away imperiously. I walked through the leaf shadows on the floor to the doorway, nodded at Miss Knowles and held up my hands to show her I had no books with me, went through the turnstile, feeling its wooden baton stroke my flesh, and stood at the wire-mesh fence outside, surveying the trees and the grass and the red-brick shirt factory beyond. Boucher. I had never heard the name before. I had never seen a nude before. Her flesh was solid, but so replete with light. Irene Mackey, from the Lecky Road, whom I had long fancied and thought beautiful, suddenly seemed ordinary.

Every week, I went back but I didn't see the woman in the painting again; Joe was often there and he began to walk out of the library with me and stroll in the park. His aim was, he said, to give me a little of the education I so sorely lacked but at least had the decency to want. The walk usually consisted of a descent down a flight of broad steps to an ornamental pond surrounded by iron railings. We would stop there, lean on the railings and look at the green-black water shifting under its carpet of water lilies. Most of the time, the water looked metallic, but on occasion, when the sun shone, it became less burnished and softened to a sexual velveteen. Joe leaned in close to my ear and half-whispered, half-shouted a garbled mess of things — stories, questions, conundrums. Sometimes his false teeth shifted in and out; sometimes he seemed unaccountably close to tears; mostly, he beamed fiercely, clanking the railings with his walking stick or stomping it on the ground for emphasis. His head swung back and forth endlessly.

'Let me tell you, since you never asked, which is to your credit, or else you're very sly,' he said one day as we stood at the pond, 'why I've never let you see that painting again. You do want to know? Don't have me waste my breath.'

'Yes, I do.'

'You saw her, the woman in the painting, eh? Didn't you?'

'Yes. I saw her.'

'Beautiful, wasn't she. Did you recognise her? Eh?'

'No. How could I?'

'How could you not? She was Irish. A Mademoiselle Murphy. She had, she had . . .'

He beamed at me. '. . . sexual intercourse with the kings of France. The kings of France. Those boys knew a thing or two in that particular area, I can tell you.'

He banged his stick delightedly on the railings.

'Oh, this was long ago in the good old days. When France was France. Beautiful all right. But she was also evil. Did you see that?'

I shook my head and looked into his bright, old–young face. His eyes were red and rheumy. He caught my shirt sleeve and tugged me down towards him. His breath whined in his chest.

'I knew a man who knew that woman. Actually, my dear young friend, knew her carnally.'

'Carnally?' I queried.

'Latin, you fool,' he snarl-smiled, 'don't they even teach you Latin? *Carnis*. *Car-nis*. Flesh. Knew her in the flesh.'

'But I thought she lived long ago, in France.'

'That makes no difference. The painter lived long ago, as you say. But she . . . she was Irish. So, you see?'

This was a conundrum. I said nothing. He took out a giant white handkerchief and blew his nose, chuckled, and stowed the handkerchief away in his trouser pocket. A corner of it continued to peep out like a white mouse with a green mucus eye.

'There's a man you've seen but never noticed and he's not far from here. He's the man I mean. He never speaks.

He stands in the same place all day at a street corner and he looks up Bligh's Lane as if he had never seen it before.'

I knew the man he meant. I had noticed him. Larry McLaughlin, a relative of the Brigid in Katie's story. Now I would hear his tale.

'Now, when he was a young man, within a week of getting married, off he goes one day up Bligh's Lane towards Holywell Hill or Sheriff's Mountain. Is it not strange that the same bump of heather has two names? Have you been there?'

'Yes, often.'

The hill beyond that was the hill where Grianan stood.

'Well, which name was the first?'

'Holywell, I suppose. There'd have been a well before there was a sheriff.'

'And who was Bligh, the man Bligh's Lane is called after?'

'I don't know.'

'And you think you live here. I could expect no more. It's one thing not knowing her. No Caliban would. But the place where you go, every silly Sunday, I bet, with your daddy, and all those damned bells ringing, and the streets stiff with boredom, and you don't even know where you are. Just snuffling round like a young foal. What will become of you?'

I shrugged and stared at the white lily napkins with their spidery yellow tongues, so still they seemed glued to the water.

'And there's another thing. Why is it sad when I ask what will become of you and not sad when I ask what will you become? Is the word "of" sad?'

He took out his white mouse handkerchief and wiped his eyes. Was he crying? I thought I'd better get away, but he caught my sleeve again.

'Anyway, off goes this man – let's call him by his first name, Larry – late afternoon, up to the hill with two names, four-and-a-half miles up and four miles down if you take the short cut over the watery brook, which he did, wouldn't you know, just as it was getting dark. It was one of those -ember months, the sinking fire months.'

The pond crinkled like tin as a breeze sped across it.

'So, Larry is coming home. You know whom I mean, of course, but we'll name no names. Discretion is the better part of candour. Dear me, I don't like what's going to happen now. Crossing water at dusk is bad luck. It's tempting fate. The world on the side you leave is never the same as the world you reach. And you know what else about the watery brook?'

'Yes. It marks the border.'

'Oh, bloody clever.' He huffed for a moment. 'So, Larry did walk into one country and crossed back at dusk into the one he'd come from. Wasn't he the sorry man, he did!'

'Why, what happened? Was he shot or something?'

'Shot, my arse. How could he have been shot and be still standing there at the street corner? Am I wasting my breath? Sure no one's ever shot at the border these days, more's the pity.'

His face was flushed with anger, and his false teeth shot in and out as he sucked on his cheeks.

'He could have been wounded and then recovered. And I am listening.'

'You're quite right. That's possible. But that's not what happened. Let's proceed. No more interruptions.'

He turned round and looked up the hill towards Rosemount.

'I see the factory lights are on. It must always be dark in there. I don't think they ever clean those windows. Can you imagine what it's like in there, with all those women, rows and rows of them, turning men's shirts back and forth all the time, collars and cuffs and tails? I'd hate to hear what they say to one another about the bodies of the men that are going to wear them. Lucky for them that we do, or they'd be out of a job, the bitches. I wonder, are their hands as clean as they should be, running them up the inside of the back of the shirt and opening them up from the inside. Is this the only city in the world where men wear shirts that women's hands have been inside even before they wear them? Eh?'

He shuddered. I thought that his shirt must be very small. The women would laugh at that all right, a little thing with the broad stripes he favoured, like a miniature gaol window on a hanger. But what had happened to Larry? Joe was swirling the loose gravel with his stick. I wanted to run off but I knew I had to stay.

'So, he's on his way home, swinging along quite happily, in the last evening of his bachelorhood, the embers of his chastity finally beginning to die down. There's a woman on the road ahead of him. She turns round at the noise of his steps; she's dawdling along and gives him a smile that puts the heart across him, for she's the most beautiful woman he has ever seen. She asks if he would walk into town with her for she's afraid of the dark. In ten or twenty yards, she's linked his arm and in half a mile, after pressing against him and sweet-talking him, they're in a field, and she's lying under him, and he's pulling at his shirt and trousers, and she's in the black grass pulling him down when – wham! She's gone!'

'How do you mean, gone?'

'Gone, for God's sake, and he was left like a man doing press-ups and the smell under him was like burnt toffee and there was smoke round his crotch. Gone.'

I laughed, embarrassed, for I really didn't know exactly what was supposed to happen, and maybe being gone was part of it – although she seemed to have left very early. But the smoke and the toffee smell? I had heard nothing of that.

Joe was bent over his stick, jabbing at the gravel; his chin was so low on his chest that it appeared, for a moment, that his head had slipped.

'When Larry got up, he was pulling his clothes together and crying and looking all around him. Over at the hedge, across the field from him, he saw a fox standing looking at him. It was still as a statue. Then it put up its head and barked.'

'A fox?'

'A fox. It was her. He ran out of that field and started running for the lights of the Lone Moor Road. Every couple of hundred yards or so, the fox would appear again in front of him, until just short of the first street lamp it disappeared, and Larry was able to get down the street and in home. He was babbling. They got the doctor, put him to bed; his fiancée came and all the relatives, neighbours, everyone, and the priest was sent for. He heard Larry's confession and gave him the last rites. When he came out of Larry's room, the priest went straight up to the fiancée, took her aside, told her the marriage was off, that she was to forget Larry, that Larry would never marry, could never have children, would never know a woman in his whole life. So there. That's the story of poor Larry.'

'And that's why he never talks but stands there looking up Bligh's Lane where it all happened?'

'That's right.'

We were both silent.

'But the priest,' I ventured, 'he couldn't have told anything if he had heard it in confession.'

'He didn't have to; Larry was raving for weeks after. It all came out. People sat around listening and crossing themselves and crying.'

Joe clattered his stick up and down on the railings. It was almost dark by now. The factory lights were on full; they must be working overtime there. The library windows were blazing too.

'But I thought you said she was the woman in the painting? Did he recognise her, tell everyone it was Mademoiselle Murphy?'

Joe looked up at me in surprise.

'What are you raving about? What woman? What painting? Larry never saw a painting in his life.'

'But you said he had carnal knowledge of that woman, the King of France's woman.'

'Christ, go home and stick to your stupid football. Never let me see you near that art room again or I'll report you. Your have a dirty mind. What woman? Carnal knowledge. What would you know, you dirty-minded scut?'

He banged his stick against the railings, and I jumped back as he snarled at me, his false teeth coming right out on their pink shield, and his face folding in. Then he sucked them back again in a flash and stomped off round the pond, struck uphill towards the factory, waving his stick and talking furiously to himself. The clouds above the factory were rolling high for thunder. Even as I ran up the steps and past the shining library windows, the first growlings came and the heavy drops of rain made exclamation marks all over my shirt. I was soaked long before I got home.

MATHS CLASS

November 1951

Every morning, at nine o'clock sharp, he came rushing into the room, his soutane swishing, his face reddened as if in anger, his features oddly calm. We would be ready with the thick tome of algebra open at the right page and as many questions as possible prepared in advance. He spoke nasally but smilingly. He had tight curls and glasses; but for the redness, he could have looked harmless. His name was Gildea.

He sat at the high desk, raised on a platform above the class. He lifted his chin, closed his eyes and chanted:

'Mental algebra. Ground rules. Well-known, but must be repeated, first for the sake of the brain-dead and the memory-less, who are in the usual staggering majority; second as a warning to those more fortunately endowed, but who take a litigant's pleasure in claiming that they have not been told, that they do not know, that the rules are not clear. I lie awake at night, imagining for these creatures a condign punishment; yet I have failed. Does this bespeak in me a failure of imagination, or in them an unanswerable corruption? You may answer the question, McConnellogue.'

'I'm afraid I cannot, Father,' replied McConnellogue automatically. This was routine.

'Your sorrow is touching. Perhaps you do not realise the importance of the question. Harkin, be so good as to inform McConnellogue what a litigant is.'

'A litigant is a person who creates disturbances by abuse of the rule of law, Father.'

'Do you agree with that superb definition, McConnellogue?'

'Absolutely, Father.'

90

'You are not litigious, McConnellogue, are you?'

'No, Father.'

'I shall test you in that statement. Are you more literate or more numerate as a consequence of my loving care, five times a week, forty minutes per time, McConnellogue?'

'I am equally blessed in both respects, Father.'

'Would you say that McConnellogue will go far, Heaney?'

'I would, Father.'

'Under what conditions would you say so, Heaney?'

'Under the conditions imposed by the question, Father.'

'Are you conversant with these conditions, Duffy?'

'I am, Father.'

'What's your name, Duffy?'

'Duffy, Father.'

'Glad to hear it. Now, ground rules. We have here, in this venerable textbook, forty simple sums in algebraic form, to each of which there is only one correct answer. There are, in this room, forty boys. One sum for each. The coincidence is pleasing. We begin with Johnson, the strange-looking creature in the left-hand corner of the front row. He gives the answer to number one in no more than two seconds. If he takes longer, he will be deemed to have given a wrong answer. McDaid, the object next to Johnson, takes number two, and so on throughout the whole zoo-like assemblage we, in our politeness, call a class. However, if Johnson is, in McDaid's considered opinion, wrong in number one, he, McDaid, does number one over again and gives the correct answer. If the person next to McDaid happens to believe that Johnson was right in number one, and McDaid wrong to correct him, he skips number two and does number three; whereupon McDaid must, if he agrees with this verdict, re-do number two. Equally, the person next to McDaid also has the choice to believe that both Johnson and McDaid were wrong in number one; if he takes this choice, he does number one over again. And so on. The choice enriches as one proceeds, so that by the time we reach that evolutionary cul-de-sac named Irwin at the back of the class, the choice will be veritably kaleidoscopic. If any sum is done wrongly by any preceding student, whether that be immediately or more distantly preceding, the student who observes this must do that sum correctly. If a sum is done incorrectly, the punishment is a mere two strokes. If a sum done correctly is incorrectly corrected, the punishment is four strokes. If the whole class misses a sum incorrectly answered, homework is doubled. If it misses more than one sum incorrectly answered, homework is doubled for the number of nights corresponding to the number of missed incorrect answers. If every sum is answered correctly, the sun will stand still in the heavens, and I will take up the teaching of a secure and sure subject, like religion. Right. Johnson, proceed. Two seconds from now!'

Johnson began.

'X equals minus two.'

McDaid followed.

'X equals three.'

It went round, very fast. The row in front of me was into it now. Suddenly, Gildea intervened.

'What number are you doing, Harkin?'

'Number thirteen, Father.'

'Fair enough. You evidently believe that number twelve was correctly answered?'

Harkin hesitated.

'Yes, Father.'

'Fair enough. Your decision. Next man. Two seconds only.'

'X equals four.'

'What number was that?'

'Number twelve, Father.'

'You consider it was wrongly answered, then?'

'Yes, Father.'

'So Harkin should have done it again?'

'Yes, Father.'

'Harkin?'

'I believe number twelve was correct, Father.'

'And with that, all preceding number twelve, otherwise you would have repeated one of them?'

'Yes, Father.'

'Next man. Not you, Molloy. You have just corrected Harkin. The squalid thing beside you. Is it alive?'

'I am, Father.' This was O'Neill.

'No exaggerations. Just give me your answer.'

'X equals five, Father.'

'And that is the answer to . . . ?'

'Number thirteen, Father.'

'Ah. So Harkin was wrong to have done number thirteen and wrong in having done it?'

'Just wrong in the answer he gave to it, Father.'

'Then number twelve was, in your opinion, done correctly?'

'Yes, Father.'

'Then Molloy was wrong in correcting number twelve?'

'Yes, Father.'

'So why did you not do number twelve again?'

'It had already been done correctly, Father.'

'But the man preceding you had done it wrongly? Ground rules state you correct the preceding error, right?'

'Yes, Father.'

'Did you?'

'No, Father, but . . . '

'Quiet! What number are you going to do now?'

'Number twelve, Father.'

'Answer?'

'X equals four.'

'This was a correction of Molloy? Yes?'

O'Neill had blundered and knew it. He just nodded.

'Molloy, your answer was "four", was it not?'

'Yes, Father.'

'But that was wrong, I'm told. Now it's right. Where are we here? Is this mathematics or is it chaos?'

Silence. Gildea smiled.

'The difference should be discernible, even to you people. Duffy, proceed, unravel the mess.'

'X equals two.'

'What number was that the answer to?'

'Number one, Father.'

'You think the first sum was wrong?'

'Yes.'

'Yes, what?'

'Yes, Sir.'

'Sir? Sir? Have I altered in appearance? Has my Roman collar become a tie, my soutane a suit of mouldy tweed?'

'No, Sir.'

'You insist on "Sir"?'

'Yes, Father.'

The class tittered and then went still.

'A spark of wit; I enjoy that. It cannot go unpunished, of course. But to the point. The first sum was wrong, you say. So all since that have been wrong?'

'Technically, yes, Sir.'

'Technically? Ah, a litigant speaks.'

'Just ground rules, Sir.'

'Were they, or were they not, wrong?'

'Some were wrong in themselves, Sir. Some were wrong in that they were done before number one was corrected, Sir.'

'Wonderful. A true litigant. You're sure of yourself, Duffy?'

'Absolutely, Sir.'

'Right. Let's start all over again. First man, first sum.'

'X equals minus two.'

'You stand by that?'

'Yes, Father.'

'Duffy was wrong then?'

'Yes, Father.'

'All this trouble for nothing, then?'

'Yes, Father.'

'All agree?'

'Yes, Father.' A chorus.

'Right, Duffy. Compute your error. One wrong answer – two strokes. One correct answer, "corrected" wrongly by you – four strokes. Eleven perfectly correct or undisputed answers cancelled by you on the grounds that they should not have been given when, in fact, they should have – forty-four strokes. Waste of time, six strokes. Playing the professional litigant, twelve strokes. Insolent mode of address, ten strokes. Moment of wit, six strokes. Can you add that?'

'Eighty-four.'

'Eighty-four what?'

'Eighty-four strokes, Sir.'

'Right. We're getting somewhere. You can add, you are learning your catechism, you are about to learn a lesson about the overweening confidence that has always marked you and your ilk. What is it that this soothes my heart like?'

'Balm, Sir.'

'A correct answer at last. Out you come.'

'No, Sir. I was right. They are wrong.'

'Oh, my. Oh, my. Duffy's right, everyone else is wrong. I see storm-clouds gather. I see apocalypse threaten. We are all innumerate but Duffy. Harkin, do that sum again, on the blackboard this time. So we can all see.'

Harkin scrawls on the blackboard.

'Can you refute that, Duffy?'

'No, Sir.'

'It's the correct answer?'

'Yes, Sir. To the wrong sum.'

'The wrong sum? THE WRONG SUM? This is ecstatic. You surpass yourself. Explain, we're all agog.'

'I'm doing section B, Sir. Everyone else is doing section A.'

'And why do you choose B, when we all choose A?'

'Because we did Section A yesterday, Sir. I assumed you did not want us to repeat what we already knew.'

'Anyone else remember our doing Section A?'

'Yes, Sir.' A chorus.

'Did I specify Section B, Duffy?'

'No, Sir, but you did not specify Section A either.'

'How many strokes do I owe you, Duffy?'

'None, Sir.'

'Your opinion, not mine. Class, stay in your seats. Do nothing. First boy I see do anything useful, two strokes. Duffy, leave the class. Class, homework doubled. Duffy, homework quadrupled.'

He hunched over his desk, glaring. The door closed quietly behind Duffy. We stared into mid-air.

SERGEANT BURKE

May 1952

Rory Griffin and I were totally enclosed within a circle of six of them. Willie Barr, their leader, kept licking the side of his mouth with his thick tongue. He was stones heavier than us; older, much tougher. He held his fist out to let Griffin see the pennies lodged between his clenched fingers. 'That's what you're going to get hit with,' he snarled. 'And then you.' He showed me his fist. Griffin first, because he was bigger. He pointed to his smaller comrades, telling them in what order they would hit us. Griffin was white with fear. I supposed I was too. There was a tremble in the back of my legs that really sickened me, for I knew it meant I wouldn't even be able to make a decent attempt to run. They were too close anyway. Griffin went down at the first blow, his face cut round the mouth. He was crying as Barr pulled him up for the next blow. Someone called: 'Cops!' and tersely Barr said, 'Everybody sit down, in a circle. Pretend to laugh at something.' I was pulled down with them as the police car moved slowly along the road twenty yards away. The passenger window was down, and the policeman was looking out. It was Sergeant Burke, getting a lift home from the Lecky Road barracks. 'Don't either of you move,' warned Barr. 'Griffin, don't you try to look round.' Griffin was still sobbing quietly and looking at the blood smear on his hand where he had wiped his mouth. I looked at Barr's forearms and heard the pennies jingle in his palm. I moved and felt a stone rub the inside of my leg, snaffled it, jumped up and threw it as hard as I could at the car, now almost past. The stone bounced on the car boot and struck the rear window. 'Holy fuck,' shouted Barr as the car reversed in a whine and everyone ran, including Griffin. I stayed where I was. I couldn't move. The tremor in the back of my legs had gone, but now I felt my feet were melting in my boots. The driver of the police car, a young constable, was upon me already, and Burke was leaning on the car door, a few feet away. The constable grabbed my shoulder and might have cuffed me if Burke had not said, very casually, 'Just bring him over here, Constable. He'll walk over himself.' I did and stood between them. Burke heaved himself off the side of the car, strolled round to the back, looked at the window, fingered the little chip mark the stone had made in the glass and the flake of paint it had loosened on the boot. 'Now why did you do a thing like that, sonny?' he asked in an almost soothing voice. I said nothing. Although I had my back to them, I knew Barr and the others were watching from the top of the back field. 'Beat the shit out of him,' shouted one. Burke stared up at them. 'Nice friends you've got there. You want to give me their names? Constable, get out your notebook and write in it.' Burke gestured towards them and brought his face close to mine. 'I don't care, you understand, if you give me their names or not. I know every one of them. Willie Barr, for instance. Seamus Greene. Just write those names down, Constable. You, sonny, I know you don't want to talk. I understand that. You can just nod your head, that's right, isn't it?'

I nodded. That was co-operation enough for Barr.

'Fuckin' stooly. Just like your uncle, like the whole lot o' ye,' shouted Barr. Burke clucked his tongue, opened the back door and half-ushered, half-pushed me in on the black leathery seats. 'Drive on, Constable,' he said, getting in beside me. 'My tea's getting spoilt. We'll give this wee lad a walk home to teach him a lesson. All right, son?' 'Fuck off,' I muttered and the constable turned round angrily. Burke laughed and restrained him. 'No, no. We can't hit the wee lad; that'd make a hero of him. Just what he wants. Right, son?' He squeezed my thigh with his hand, leaving brief white pressure points on my flesh. 'Drive nice and slow, up his street, this one, to the top, then turn left.' I saw women standing at the doors, talking, as they always did, and the men lounging around the street lamp at the corner, smoking their thin cigarettes. Their faces followed the car as it lazed up the steep street. Burke was smiling towards me and waving his notebook in the air. But he wasn't saying a word, just staring at me out of his red, fleshy face.

'Stop it here, Constable,' he commanded when we were passing the door of Barr's house. He got out, knocked on the door, talked to Mrs Barr when she answered, pointed towards me in the back of the car. She glared past him at me. He went two doors up, to Greene's house, did the same. Then to the house of two others from the gang, each time pointing towards me, sitting stranded in the back seat. We drove on when he got in, stopped at his house near the cemetery. He turned to me.

'This is your second time in a police car, isn't that right?'

I nodded. Burke had been in charge the night they had searched the house for the pistol and interrogated us in the barracks.

'Well, now, weren't we the easygoing men to let your daddy go the last time? A gun in the house and him with the brother he had? His big brother, Eddie. Did you ever wonder about that, or ask him why? Ever ask yourself why? For some others must have wondered, if you didn't.'

I said nothing.

'Now Barr, that big slag, he thinks he knows why. I'll do you one favour. I'll tell you this – Barr's got it wrong. I'd say your daddy has it wrong too. Maybe you should ask your mother, now her daddy's got sick – none too soon either. Still, there you are. Once an informer, always an informer. That's what they'll say. And we'll see what comes out in the wash, eh? Off you go.'

He pushed me out before him and waved me away. I walked across the Lone Moor towards home. I could see no way out. No one would believe me; or if they could see what had really happened, they'd still be doubtful. Because

99

of Eddie. Wasn't that what Burke was saying? Yes. But also no. For Barr had got it wrong, he had said. But how could my father be wrong about his own brother and a policeman be right? And what did my mother know that was different? I'd have to run away, I thought. Chicago? The name ran senselessly in my head. My face felt as though it had set into a hard plaster mask, although I was crying inside, hard and dry, but crying.

INFORMER

June 1952

The first time I ran away after that, I got as far as the gangplank of the Belfast-to-Liverpool boat. Then my father and Tom appeared with a plain-clothes policeman and took me home in Tom's car. I had a shilling and sixpence in my pocket and no raincoat. Liam was embarrassed when he heard that. *No raincoat?* he echoed, disbelievingly. The second time, I got a lift in a lorry that left me outside the village of Feeney, no more than a dozen miles away, and I had to give up and walk home to more uproar and a stricter regime. After that second attempt, I was no longer allowed to go to the public library and borrow books. Weekdays I went to school, weekends I stayed in, no matter what the weather. My mother never let up.

'What could have possessed you to go running to those vermin? Have you no self-respect, no pride? And if you've none for yourself, have you none for the rest of us? Thank God my father's too ill to hear about this – the shame alone would finish him. A grandson of his going to the police!'

'I didn't go to the police. I threw a stone at them.'

'Same thing in the circumstances. God alone knows why this sort of thing keeps happening. Is it a curse? What did we do to deserve this?'

'What sort of thing?'

'The police, the police! That sort of thing, you helpless gom.'

My father asked me over and over to tell him in detail what Sergeant Burke had said. I didn't mention anything about Burke's reference to the earlier interrogation, or why they had let him go, or his mentioning Eddie or Grandfather, or hinting I should ask my mother. Why didn't I take a few punches from Barr and his gang? My father wanted to know this. It would all have been over now. Didn't I know what sort of people the police were? Had I no guts, no sense, no savvy, no shame? His face flushed and his reddish hair shivered above his ears when he leaned towards me and my breath touched him.

The police had stopped visiting houses in the street and asking questions. It was all a put-up job. They could not have cared less; they were just making trouble. Or rather, Burke was making trouble. He knew everything, it seemed, and was twisting the knife again in a casual sort of way. I knew that it had to do with my grandfather, who had fallen seriously ill recently and was not expected to live much more than a year. Maybe his approaching death had stirred a memory in Burke. Meanwhile, I was out of it. No one would play football with me. If I watched a game and kicked the ball back from the sideline, the player would lift the ball and wipe it on the grass before going on with the throw-in.

So, I didn't take a few punches. Now what *would* it take? I asked my father that.

'A bit of sense. And a bit of courage.'

That angered me. 'Courage? To get battered? That's just stupidity.'

'And what do you think this is? Eh? What's this? Everybody has to suffer just because you couldn't face it.'

He was right but he was wrong too. One night he said it again. I was listening to a wireless report on the Korean War and looking at the map of Korea in the newspaper, running my fingers across the thirty-ninth parallel and imagining the Americans retreating down the peninsula before the North Koreans and the Chinese. Somebody had insulted him that day on my account. Why hadn't I taken a few punches? Why did I have to bring the police back into our lives? Was once not enough? First, the gun. Now this. Was there something amiss with me? No, I told him, there's something amiss with the family. The police were on top of

102

us long before I was born. If he wanted to blame someone, let him blame Eddie, not me.

He hit me so fast, I saw nothing. My shoulder felt hot and broken.

I got up, hating him, although I could feel the tears coming as the pain increased through the numbness.

I saw that Liam had closed his eyes and that my mother had stopped cutting the loaf of bread on the deal table. The knife lay there, with crumbs still sticking to its saw-edge. The half-cut slice leaned out sadly from the squat loaf. She had her back to us, and I saw the sigh run the length of her spine, down from the shoulders. Her apron string stretched. My father looked at me, his face suddenly sad as well as angry. He was sorry he had hit me; but he wanted to hit me again. He stood up from his chair and said very quietly to my mother, touching her shoulder as though he were picking a loose hair from her dress:

'I'm going to clip some of those roses. They're in bad need of it.'

He went out to the garden. The latch clicked as he closed the door behind him. She turned round, her eyes shining and pale with anger.

'Bed,' she said, 'bed, right now.'

'But I've had no dinner.'

'Bed, this instant!'

I fled upstairs.

ROSES

July 1952

There was a pickaxe in the shed, a great bow of iron on an oiled shaft. I brought it out and drove it as hard as I could into the soil near a rose bush. The bush trembled, and a few petals fell. I drove it in again in a full arc, and this time felt the point strike at roots. A third time, and the roots yielded more, and the bush shook in the sun's glare. I turned the pickaxe round in my hands and used the blunter end. This time, the root gave way, and I had to prise the pickaxe out by shifting it back and forth in the soil. Then I went on, round both sides of the bush, until it sagged sideways, and the petals were shining crimson all over the path and glinting weakly in the disturbed earth.

I hunched down for a moment to watch a sleeve of greenfly tighten on a rose stem. I counted the black spots on the leaves, fingering the shiny stubs of the thorns that sharpened to so fine a point that only a prick of blood on my finger told me exactly where the sharpness ended. The heat was like a nausea. I pulled away a diseased leaf, and rose petals came out into the air with the tug. I shook the rose bush, and more petals fluttered down. I crushed some in my hand and sniffed the satiny scraps of colour, but they had no aroma. Yet, growing, they gave off this powerful odour that felt to me like dread, a hot radar signal.

I was soaked in sweat. There were ten more rose bushes in a staggered line down to the gate, and five more at the sun-trap at the side of the shed. I would never have the strength to uproot them all. I went back to the shed and dragged out two bags of cement, threw them on the ground and punctured them with the pickaxe in one powdery stroke. It was easy to tear the paper back, get a spade and shovel the white powder over each bush, beating them as flat as I could with the back of the spadehead, sending petals and cement dust whirling in spirals with each blow. It was only when I saw the cement bags lying flat and torn on the path that I stopped to survey what I had done. The heat had lessened by now. My father would be home in little more than an hour. In a panic, I grabbed the bags and folded them, thrust them back in the shed, took out the yard brush and began to sweep the petals and dry powder into the rose beds, thinking I would have the path clean at least. But as the nausea and dread died in me and I saw the broken roses hanging down in the choking dust, I gave up and stood there in a trance, hearing the front door open and my mother's voice and the children babbling and running. They all came right out to the yard, shouting for me, my mother right behind them, smiling. Then they all went still; I blinked at them through the dust that was making my eyes smart. They kept appearing over and over again as in a series of snapshots, all of them posed at different angles. My mother's hand was at her heart. I walked straight to her and past her. She put out her hand and clutched my bare arm.

'In the name of all that's sacred . . . ' she began, the tears rolling down her cheeks, 'what have you done? What has possessed you to do such a thing?'

'Ask Father. He'll know.' I replied.

I felt such fury then, I could have done it all over again and only the sight of the shocked faces of my younger brothers and sisters stopped me going down the path and picking up the spade or the pickaxe and beating the roses even flatter. It occurred to me at the same moment that Eilis wasn't there. Could she have been upstairs watching, too frightened to come down, while all this was going on? And Liam would run his hands through his red hair and roll his eyes and then throw his arms wide in helplessness. And my father, I thought, through my mother's wailing and sobbing, which was relentless now, he could go fuck himself. I clumped angrily up the stairs, stripped naked, got into bed

105

and lay there waiting. After a few minutes, a vibration started up in me, and my head twitched in a sort of dry grief. Then it stopped, and I lay there watching the shadows on the ceiling lengthen, waiting for my father.

That autumn, I would start secondary school and was enchanted by the notion that I would be reading new languages – especially Latin and French. I was trying to read a prose translation of *The Aeneid*, but the strange English and the confusion of names left me stranded. I had left my Virgil, I realised, lying open on the table. I closed my eyes and tried to remember some of the names: Turnus. Nisus and Euryalus, Aeneas himself, Turnus, Anchises. The same names repeated themselves. I could remember no more. I opened my eyes and my father was looking at me from the door.

He said nothing. He looked. He moved inside the room and closed the door. The skin on my belly crawled, and my thighs were slick. I didn't want to look at him, but his eyes held mine and, as he moved again, my head followed him.

'So I know, do I?'

I nodded.

'Tomorrow, and the day after, and the day after that, and every other day that comes, you'll know.'

He walked out of the room, slamming the door behind him. I lay there all night. The others slept downstairs. The house was perfectly still. I couldn't hear voices. I wanted desperately to go to the bathroom but couldn't go down the stairs. Hot and twisted with discomfort, I somehow fell asleep.

When I woke, I had to pull on trousers and bolt to the bathroom, through the kitchen and scullery. It was already mid-morning. To my astonishment, my father was there with my uncles, my mother's brothers. They stopped talking as I fled through the kitchen and remained silent until I had returned and gone up the stairs again. My mother was nowhere to be seen; I guessed she had gone over to see Katie, who lived only two streets away, to seek advice and comfort. I didn't know what to do, so I got back into bed and listened to the murmur of voices. There was a noise of men moving, a shout, and steps went down the backyard path. The gate was opened. I got up and looked out on the ruined garden and saw men carrying in bags of cement from a lorry parked at the back gate. My father and uncles went out with them, and there was much heaving and clanking before they came in again, swing-walking a cement-mixer from one side to the other. Then they brought in sand and heaped it in a cone beside the cement-mixer and buckets. All day long, as my father and Tom mixed cement, Dan and John spread it, while the other workmen uprooted and cleared the rose bushes ahead of them, raking the ground level as they went and throwing the dead bushes into the back of the lorry. By three in the afternoon, they were finished. The yard glistened grey all down one side and on the other side of the shed that I could not see from the window. They cased the wet cement in planks, cleaned up and left. I think that was the first time my father ever missed a day's work.

Again, I slept alone that night. No food was offered, and I didn't ask for any. Next day, the newly cemented section had whitened. I saw Liam removing the planks that had cased it. At that point, I dressed and went downstairs. My mother turned away when I came into the kitchen and went out to the scullery. Liam came in, shook his head at me and put his finger to his lips. So I got myself some bread and butter and tea and made to go out. My mother came in from the scullery.

'Upstairs,' she said pointing. I saw the Virgil sitting on top of the radio, grabbed it and went upstairs. When my father came in at dinner-time, Gerard and Eamon were sent up to tell me I could come down to eat. Everyone was sitting round the table, silent. All the children were ashamed for me. We ate in silence. At the end of the meal, my father got up to remove the plates, as he always did. I made to help him. He put his hand on my shoulder and held me to my chair.

'You ask me no more questions. Talk to me no more. Just stay out of my way and out of trouble.'

I sank back in my chair. The dishes went clattering into the scullery sink. Everybody seemed to be looking at me but their eyes did not meet mine. I returned upstairs and fell across the bed, still angry, but more horrified, and half-cried, half-cursed myself to sleep. It was getting dark when I woke. Someone had touched me. I opened my eyes a slit, stared at the wallpaper and closed them again as my father bent over me. He kissed my hair. I slowly stiffened, from the toes up. In a moment, I would cough or cry; but the bed rose as his weight lifted, and I rose lightly with it, like a wave lifting. He thought I was still asleep. He whispered to himself something I didn't catch. The bedroom door closed and the stairs creaked their old familiar music as he went down.

That more or less ended it. The yard remained concreted. When I kicked a football there, I could see it bounce sometimes where the rose petals had fallen and I would briefly see them again, staining the ground. Walking on that concreted patch where the bushes had been was like walking on hot ground below which voices and roses were burning, burning.

BISHOP

August 1952

'Go now,' said Liam, weeks later. 'And tell the Bishop.'

'How do you get to see a bishop?' I asked.

'For God's sake, go to the door of the parochial house, ring the bell and ask the housekeeper if you could see His Lordship on a private and personal matter of great urgency. Or ask if you could make an appointment to see him, at *his* convenience.'

'And what if she says no?'

'She won't say no. She'll likely tell you a time to come back at, after she has wakened the wee slob from his armchair.'

'Then what?'

'Then, idiot, the problem is to get yourself in the clear. I've been thinking about this. There's only one sure way. You have to be seen going into that police station with a priest to make your apology and be seen to come out again with him. Then, no matter what happens inside, we'll start the rumours about Burke.'

'What rumours?'

'Oh, go and get the priest in first,' he bawled. 'Just get him in. Then I'll tell you.'

Bishop Coulter held out his hand. I went on one knee and kissed the ring on his finger. He lifted his hand away, I got up, he waved me down into a chair. He sat at the end of the table, three empty chairs away. His black coat was well-tailored and sat very well, I thought, against his purple shirt. *Shirt?* What *was* its name? I had to concentrate.

'Now, my child,' he piped in a light voice that was always surprising, since it emerged from such a biscuit-barrel of a body, 'what is this private matter you wish to see me about?'

When I had finished telling him, he frowned a little and regarded me steadily and, I thought, suspiciously.

'You were very much at fault, you know that?'

'Yes, Your Lordship.'

'The police have their duties too.'

'Yes, Your Lordship.'

'And the sergeant could, you know, have ended your school career, by bringing a charge against you. Yet he did not. That puts you in his debt.'

'Yes, Your Lordship. I know that.'

'That area you live in, it does have some most unsavoury characters in it, along with good, decent Catholic people as well.'

I nodded vigorously.

'What exactly are you here for? What are you asking me to do?'

'I wondered, Your Lordship, if you might suggest to me the best way to apologise to Sergeant Burke.'

'Simply go and do so, my child. To the barracks or to his house. Tell him how genuinely sorry you are. I know him. He is a Christian man. He will accept your apology.'

'But the trouble is, Your Lordship, if I go to see him like that, everyone will think I'm informing again, that I'm going to the police to report names. If I go near him, I make my own situation worse.'

'Well, can't you write to him?'

Write to him. How could you write to a policeman? I had never written a letter in my life. Only my mother wrote letters – no, notes, to the grocer or to the rent office asking if we could have more time to pay, and would this sum of money serve in the meantime? I really liked that 'serve' and wondered where she had got it. It made handing the note over, and waiting for the man reading it, much easier. It was better language than theirs, but they would recognise it. Anyway, Liam had thought of this possibility too.

'But I would like the apology to be as public as the wrong. I feel I owe it to him and to my own conscience.'

'I see.' He drummed on the table with his fingers. There was a ghost of a smile on his face for a second.

'I must say the sergeant's idea of justice in this instance is not what I might call entirely Catholic. It's what we might call state justice. And your family has had its troubles before now. But these are delicate matters, better not gone into.'

I nodded mild assent.

'Haven't I seen you at Mass these last weeks?'

'Yes, Your Lordship. I go every day.'

'You are, I gather, doing excellently at school too.'

'As well as I can, Your Lordship.'

'All very recent, though, is it not?'

Liam had prepared me carefully for this.

'Two months and one week exactly, Your Lordship, since that incident with Bur . . . with the sergeant. I found myself very much cut off, by myself . . . '

Here I faltered. Liam had advised me to get tearful at this bit, but there was no problem. I *was* tearful. My sorrow for myself was overwhelming.

'. . . and I found myself on my own, and no one would talk to me, and it was in the church, only there, that I could be safe and it was there that I found myself able to talk.'

'Talk?'

'Yes, Your Lordship, to talk to God.'

He gazed at me for a moment. Although I had tears in my eyes, I wondered about that last sentence. Too corny?

'And has there been any, shall we say, consequence, notable consequence, of this talking to God?'

Consequence? I had to dither.

'I'm not sure, Your Lordship. All I know is that I want to, I feel at times I'd like to . . . '

'Yes, my child?'

'Devote myself, you know, think of devoting myself to the religious life.'

'You feel you have a vocation, is that it?'

111

'Yes, Your Lordship. I know I'm too young to think about this, but the . . . '

'You are young indeed. Still, vocations are deeply rooted. You must nurture this. But make no decisions as yet. When you're older, you'll know. The conviction, when it comes, is implacable.'

There was a pause.

'Leave this to me. I'll think about it. See me again, say a year from now. I shall watch your progress at school with interest. This cloud will lift.'

He held out his hand. I went down on one knee and kissed his ring again.

'Go in peace. And pray for me.'

I bowed and left. A year from now? A year? Could it go on for a year? I shut my eyes in disbelief.

It was almost two weeks later when the parish Administrator, Father O'Neill, the Bishop's right-hand man, called to the door. My mother was at the shops and my father was at work. O'Neill was always in a hurry, always brutal. When I opened the door he pointed at me and said,

'Right, you're the boyo. You're coming with me this minute to the barracks to make an apology to Sergeant Burke. Put on your coat, if you have one. Did you never hear of a hairbrush? Never mind. Hurry. Where's your mother?'

'At the shops. She'll be back in a minute.'

'Can't wait, can't wait. Tell her afterwards. Come on now. Forget the coat.'

Liam was in the hallway behind me. He winked as I closed the door. Down the street, along the field, hurrying to keep up with O'Neill's long stride, looking back over my shoulder to see if my mother had appeared yet, to see if she was seeing this, watching Liam and a few others emerge into the back lane, looking straight at the men on the Blucher Street corner as they eyed me going past and saluted the priest, wishing there had been a football game going on so that more people could see this, reaching the barracks at the end of the lower field where the Lecky Road met our road, round the vegetable plot at the side, up the gravelled path, in the open door. A constable was leaning on the counter, talking to a plain-clothes man who had a cigarette hanging from his lip. He looked narrowly through the smoke.

'Ah,' he said, 'the Roman Catholic clergy. We're honoured.'

O'Neill glared at him.

'For your information, there's no other kind of Catholic clergy but the Roman Catholic. And I didn't come here to talk to the likes of you. Get the sergeant!'

He addressed this command to the constable, but Burke had already come out of an inner room, his face set and surprised.

'Father. Good day to you. Come on in.'

The plain-clothes man dropped his cigarette on the floor and swivelled his heel on it, eyeing O'Neill all the while. In Burke's office, O'Neill sat down promptly on a chair in front of Burke's desk, grabbed me by the elbow and held me standing alongside him. His grip was tight, and he shook me every so often as he talked. Burke, too, sat down.

'What's brought you here, Father?'

He had not looked at me so far, but he was seeing me and his mind was racing. I decided he had a knot in his stomach and that made me feel calm.

'What's brought me here, Sergeant, is a request from His Lordship, the Bishop, that this boyo here should be brought to apologise to you, and that I should hear if his apology is acceptable, or if there is anything else you should want us to know. So, if you'll be good enough to listen, he'll make his apology now.'

He shook me.

'Speak up. Apologise to the sergeant.'

Burke's eyes switched to me. His face was expressionless.

'I'm sorry, Sir, for throwing a stone at your car and damaging it. It was a wrong thing to do.'

'And you won't do it again,' prompted O'Neill, shaking me again, 'no more hooligan behaviour.'

'And I won't do it again.'

'Or anything like it,' declared O'Neill, jogging me. He was unsatisfied.

'Or anything like it.'

I could say no more. I hoped he would ask for nothing else. Or at least, nothing else before Burke said something.

Burke smiled sardonically. 'The trouble we have with that Limewood Street lot, Father. This fella, his older brother, and Barr, Moran, Harkin, Toner . . . You wouldn't believe it.'

'Indeed and I can imagine it. There's some bad boys there. But this one's not the worst of them, I'm told.'

Finally, he let go of my arm. I rubbed my elbow and stood there, not letting anything happen inside me.

'It's more than good of you, Father, to take up your valuable time for a scamp like this one. I'm sure you have other and more important things to do.'

Mistake, Burke, I said to myself. Don't tell O'Neill what he should be doing. Sure enough, O'Neill responded,

'I've plenty to do, Sergeant, as I'm sure you have yourself. And I'm not privy to all that went on. But His Lordship asked me to come here and listen to this boy's apology for reasons which he said you would well understand but which, in his wisdom, he felt no need to explain to me. So I'm sure it's a minor matter to you, but I don't have more important things to do than serving my Bishop.'

'Indeed, Father, indeed,' Burke murmured. 'Well, would you let His Lordship know that I'm sorry too that he should have been inconvenienced by this matter and that he can rest assured the incident's closed as far as we are concerned.'

'I'll do that. And I can take it you're accepting this boy's apology?'

Burke hated this. But he had nowhere to go.

'Yes. I accept it. Of course, I do. On condition he does nothing like that again.'

That was his silky voice. He looked at me again, and I quailed inwardly at the force of his glance, but held my face sombre.

O'Neill and I walked out of the station and parted at the vegetable patch. He wagged his finger at me, told me to stay clear of the riff-raff around the street corner; that I was lucky His Lordship had taken an interest in me; that I hoped I would repay it by behaving myself and becoming a decent upstanding citizen. I nodded humbly and dumbly, dying to get away, especially as a crowd of the same riff-raff had collected up the field to watch what was going on. O'Neill strode off, and I walked up towards them. They walked slowly towards me, Barr among them. They crowded round.

'What was all that about? Why was the priest in with the cops?'

'The Bishop sent O'Neill in to tell Burke off for all his lies about me. I think Burke's going to be excommunicated. The Bishop's thinking about it. Either that, or he'll have to be transferred down the country. The Bishop's written to the government about it.'

They looked at me in silence.

'Tell us what he said. What did Burke say?'

They streeled along behind me.

'O'Neill told me I wasn't to say anything more. He made Burke apologise and told me to leave it at that. Him an' the Bishop, they'll see to it from here in.'

Liam beamed at me. 'What rumours? You were asking *me*? Maybe you've caught on at last.'

Later, in the backyard of our own house, he said,

'Next time, Burke'll flatten you. Just stay out of his way an' out of trouble. Maybe you should become a priest. Give us all peace.'

I shrugged him off, laughing, and cartwheeled down the yard. Tonight, I would play football.

GRANDFATHER

October 1952

My grandmother, my mother's mother, had died when I was so small that I had to be lifted up by the side of the coffin to kiss her cold-ennobled brow. A huge pair of rosary beads was wound about her hands, and her mouth was a purple line receding under her nose. But I scarcely remembered her, except as a kind woman in black, who pulled a shawl around her shoulders in a sawing motion before she sat down and revealed a pair of laced boots under her heavy dress.

Now Grandfather was sick. Propped up in a bed that seemed to enlarge as he got smaller, he seemed always to have been crying, so red and sore were his eyes, although his skin was papery dry. I was sent to live in the house, three streets away, to help Aunt Katie who had left her own house to look after him. I resented this. It was a punishment, I knew, for all the trouble I had caused. Katie didn't mind. She was out of work permanently now. Yet she never seemed to me at ease with her father, nor he with her. There was a nervousness, even a trace of anger, in their address.

At first, I hated having to sit with Grandfather.

'Just talk about football,' Liam advised. 'He used to run the Derry and District League. Or the priests. He's good value on them, but now he's getting nervous, so he mightn't be as good as he used to be. Like Constantine.'

Great-uncle Constantine, on my mother's side, was the sole family heretic. He had been a know-all, we were told, a man who read too many books and disagreed with everybody, especially the priests. In his thirties, he started to read a notorious French writer called Voltaire, who was on the Catholic index of forbidden authors, and soon after he hung a placard on the wall of his living room, with the slogan

CRUSH THE INFAMOUS ONE painted in red on a black background; he said that was his and Voltaire's Declaration of Faith. Then he went blind, became ill and caved in by being restored to the bosom of the Church before he died. The blindness was a judgement and a warning, we were told. Thank God he had heeded it, but no wonder, for his sainted mother, Isabella – or Bella, for short – had worn out her knees praying for his soul. Lord, she was the happy woman when he died, escorted into heaven by the Last Sacraments and wee Father Gallagher from the Long Tower parish, who had personally burnt the Voltaire book page by page in the kitchen fire, saying better far that these pages should burn, like Voltaire himself, rather than the soul of the man who had read them and been blinded body and soul by their evil glare. I never saw Constantine, but he was a great name to us, the only admitted heretic, whose final collapse was a melancholy propaganda victory for the priests, who now were my teachers.

But it was Grandfather who put me right on this. I used sit at a table in his bedroom, doing homework, while he sat there against his pillows, busily dying of boredom, as far as I could see. He rarely spoke; but once he asked me what I was doing.

'Just some French exercises.'

'French! What do you want to be bothered with French for? Sure who speaks French round here? Waste of time. Fit you better to be studying Irish, your own language.'

'An' who speaks Irish round here?'

'Frankie Meenan, Johnny Harkin. That's two. And plenty more. And look at what the French did to Constantine. Lost him his sight, then, they say, his soul.'

'Constantine? Sure he died a Catholic.'

'He did not. He didn't. He died a heretic. Refused to see the priest and died holding that French book across his chest that they tried to get off him.'

'I heard diff . . .'

'Of course you did. They cooked up the story so's not

to give a bad example. But old Con, he's down there roasting with all the other atheists. God rest him.'

At that he laughed suddenly, and so did I.

'Aye, God rest him in his wee suit of fire, reading his fancy French book.'

And he laughed again, in a series of hiccups and snorts. I was so pleased for Constantine that I was shocked at myself. Then I wanted to ask Grandfather, 'What about you? Are you going to hold out?' but couldn't bring myself to it. Besides, he had suddenly gone sombre again.

'What else do they teach you up there?'

'Oh, Irish, Latin, Greek, maths, history . . . '

'History. What history?'

'Ancient history, the Romans and . . . '

'I'll be bound, it couldn't be ancient enough for that lot. There's a lot of ancient history in this town they couldn't teach and wouldn't if they could.'

'Like what?' I thrilled for a moment. Was he going to tell me something direct? Now that he was sinking, was he going to pay some attention and say something about his past, instead of standing around looking stern and looking through me, as he had always done? Was I going to hear the Billy Mahon story again now, from the mouth of the man who did him in?

'You're better not knowing.'

He jutted his lower lip out a little and glared at the blankets. I could have hit him.

'Well, that's maybe why they don't teach it at school, then.'

'Oh aye, smart boy, maybe indeed.'

He fell silent. I waited but he stayed quiet. I went back to my French grammar.

My mother came up regularly to see him, as did her brothers, Dan, Tom, Manus, John. She spent long times in the bedroom with him, while I lay on the sofa downstairs, reading, wondering how long he would take to die and when I could get back to my own house. She came down one day, pale, and sat heavily in the armchair opposite. I looked sideways at her. Her face looked broken and her hands gripped one another in her lap. I asked her, was anything wrong, but she shook her head and tightened her lips in a way that reminded me of Grandmother's dead mouth. It was easy to know that something had been said upstairs between her and her father but I was reluctant to leave it at that. I pretended to read for a minute or two but then she began to shake and cry and I got up to put my arm round her and soothe her. She cried and cried, the whole top half of her body shuddering. I wanted to say something about her father really wanting to die, to join his wife in the other world, and all that guff the older people went in for, but I knew that was not where her grief lay. She groaned, bent over as though her stomach ached, straightened up and looked me straight in the face, her tears streaming.

'Eddie,' she said, 'dear God, Eddie. This will kill us all.'

His name boomed in my ears and my whole nervous system jumped and stood out before me like a constellation.

'*Eddie?*'

'Shhshhshh,' she whispered, shaking her head. 'Not a word, not a word. Don't listen to me. I'm just upset at Grandfather's dying up there.'

After a bit, she straightened up, went out to the scullery and bathed her face, though her eyes were still red, and told me I wouldn't have to stay much longer, that they'd soon take him into the hospital for treatment and that he'd never come out of it alive, and I'd soon be home again with everybody else.

'He's beginning to wander a bit in his mind. Pay no attention to what he says and don't, whatever you do, don't repeat it. Not even to me.'

She went off. That was the beginning of her long trouble. I stayed there, Grandfather upstairs, the house darkening, Aunt Katie not yet returned, my heart haunted by tremors.

DEATHBED

November 1952

Grandfather wanted me to read the newspaper to him, page by page, starting with the sport. Even the horse-racing seemed to interest him, although he had never been a gambler himself. Then the news. Then the death notices. When we had exhausted the paper he asked me to talk to him about what I was doing, about school, my friends, life on the street, home. I asked him about what it had been like working for the *Derry Journal* in the twenties and thirties as a linotype operator, about his fight to get the workers unionised, about the troubles of the twenties, about professional football and boxing. I wanted him to tell me the story I had heard in fragments from the stairs, when I was a youngster, and from Brother Regan's sermon. But he would not yield on the Billy Mahon episode; he'd just say those were bad times and some things were best forgotten except that we had to keep up the fight against the government, always, always.

'What's wrong with my mother?' I asked him one day, for she had just left and was shaky and upset every time she came.

Oh, he replied, she had her troubles but she'd be all right. Why does she keep talking about Eddie? I asked him, lying, for she had never mentioned him at all since that one occasion, now two weeks back. He roused himself at that and pretended to wonder too, but was uneasy and asked me what she had said. Only his name, I told him, and that there was something terrible. But Eddie was my father's brother and was long since disappeared, so what could it be now? What could she know now that had begun to trouble her?

120

But she had sworn me to silence, I told him, for she knew she could talk to me and I would say nothing.

'Not even to your father?'

I knew to say it.

'Especially not to my father. She said that. But I shouldn't even talk to you about it; it's only that I'm worried about her.'

I pressed and pressed through long afternoons until he tired and slept and Katie came to shoo me away and let me go back to my family, sometimes overnight, for I was getting too pale and too bound up with him. Even though my mother was beginning to be ill by this time, and visiting my grandfather less and less, I still longed to get back to him, to keep at him until he told me what was going on, what had happened. I was getting nowhere when the priests intervened.

Father Moran arrived in the bedroom one afternoon, escorted by Katie, his bright stole over his shoulders and a little box in his hand. Katie was bearing a lit candle in one hand and a bowl of water in the other, with a white napkin draped over her arm. I should have realised this was going to happen, for the room had practically been fumigated that morning, despite Grandfather's protests.

'Father, here's Father Moran to have a chat with you . . . ' Katie began.

He was one of the hearty priests.

'Sure, the man doesn't need me. I thought you said he wasn't well, Katie? You're the picture of health, Mr Doherty. But now that I'm here, I might as well . . . '

Grandfather had moved in the bed with a kind of terror. Pointing at Katie, he quavered, 'Get that man out of here. When I want a priest, I'll ask for one, not before. Get him out.'

'Och, Mr Doherty, c'mon now, this is just a friendly visit . . . Listen, son,' bending towards me, 'you run along downstairs now. Off you go.'

He pushed me in the back.

'Let that wee fella stay here. Katie Doherty, I'll never forgive you this. Bringing him in like this without warning.'

I was pushed out, and the door closed. I stood there to listen, but the priest opened the door again, raised his finger and said, 'Off you go, downstairs, until you're called for.' I went down and listened to the sound of voices: Katie's, Father Moran's, Grandfather's scarcely audible. There was movement of chairs on the floor above and then a silence. Katie and Father Moran came down the stairs. She was distressed, and he was slightly flushed. They came into the kitchen, and again I was told to get out, this time to the backyard from where I could see them through the window, standing in the middle of the kitchen, talking. Father Moran left, and Katie called me in to tell me she had to go down to my mother's straight away, and I was to sit with Grandfather who was, Christ knows, a heathen if ever there was one, and she didn't know what she could do, with the disgrace and the shame of it, the things he said on his deathbed to the good priest, Sweet Heart of Jesus, what was to be done? She bustled into her overcoat and went off.

Grandfather was shaking. That bitch of a daughter. That black-avised priest. Those vultures, waiting for your strength to ebb and coming in to claim you and frighten everybody else left alive with their victory. Now he knew what Constantine had gone through. Sure when he needed them, they were no use to him. When he fought for Ireland, who condemned them more? What was the hold they had over the women anyway? And on and on. I was horrified at what he had done but the horror was striped with pride. He was holding out. But he was exhausted.

'Don't let them get me at the last moment, son. Don't let them.'

'No. I won't,' I answered, having no idea how I could stop them.

'Promise. Ah, how can a child like you promise? What can you do?'

'I'll warn you if I know they're coming.'

He half-smiled at that and reached out for my hand. I held his, for he had no strength, and it was thus that he fell asleep.

LUNDY BURNS

December 1952

So his last days began. I listened to him talk, went deaf, listened. At first, there was nothing but lament. Then there was admiration for my father as a boxer and the night he won the Northwest championship with a blow in the last round when he was miles behind on points, his eyes cut and closed, his nose broken. I knew that, but heard it again in smaller detail. He described how he cleaned his linotype machine after the night shift, leaving it gleaming; how the smell of ink still reminded him of the basement darkness he walked into every night, especially noticeable when it was summery and bright outside. How he could tell if his wife, Lizzie, my grandmother, was hiding something from him because he knew her breathing so well, as if he had a stetho-scope to her breast – when she was worried there was always a throb visible in her left temple – and how ashamed he was he had not let her see how he loved knowing her like that, watching her tenderly behind his husband's mask.

One Friday night, when I was longing to get back home for the white fish soup my mother always made and the weekly comic-cuts from Uncle Phonsie's shop, Grandfather came out of a long, chest-heaving sleep and looked wildly about him. It was the eighteenth of December. Raindrops, high-lighted, were sliding in slant ocelli across the windowpane. Lundy, I knew, would soon be burning in effigy from the stone pillar above the city walls, on the hill opposite. The pillar was topped by a statue of Governor Walker, the defender of the city in the siege of 1689; Lundy, the traitor, swung always on the hero's pillar, a hanged giant, exploding in flame to the roll of drums from the massed bands below, out of sight behind the walls, although their banners poked up and fluttered in the stone-wet dark. We would watch for the moment when Lundy's crotch exploded in a burst of rockets that streaked away in several directions at once. Then the flames climbed on him with sudden avarice. Christmas felt close from then.

I propped Grandfather up in bed. 'He's lost the will to live.' That was the whisper among his sons and daughters, who had sat so often by him, looking at him intently but talking about him as if he wasn't there. He lay there in a collarless, cream-coloured simmet that exposed the scrawniness of his throat and threw his severe features into relief. He looked at and through me at such times. To his children, he was both pathetic and autocratic, crumpled and unforgiving as he lay there, not losing his power to those around him but drawing it back into himself, taking it away with him, reefing it round him like a sheet. To me, this was beginning to look like what they meant in religious class when they spoke of a soul in torment.

This evening, he didn't know where he was when I switched on a bedside light. He groaned, looked around wildly for a moment. Then he settled. In the ensuing silence, I heard the first rolls of the Orange bands swell, the drums in a long rallentando. 'Close that window, for Christ's sake,' he said suddenly, 'I don't want to hear those savages with their tom-toms.' The window was closed, but I pretended to close it again so that I could look out across the house tops to the huge figure lolling on the pillar, flames crawling upward from his feet. I turned round to catch the tail of Grandfather's anger as it disappeared into his eyes. For a moment, he had looked threatening.

There was a flaw in the air. I felt it enter me as I breathed, and it made my heart murmur a little frantically before I could exhale it. His face before me altered from Roman-calm to puckered; he was odourless as a statue lying there that night, although usually I could smell his old age, like the tang of alcohol degrading in the clean air. The drums rolled loud and then were stifled as we exchanged looks, and my instincts rose to the bait that had so often been withdrawn just as I reached it.

'Only your mother knows it all. I had to tell someone, especially her, but now I'm sorry. She can't understand, she can't forgive, and I don't want forgiveness from the likes of Moran.'

Eddie was dead, he told me as the drums rolled and rolled again. He had been executed as an informer. An informer. And I had thought that Eddie had got away. But my father knew; that's what he knew. That his brother was an informer. Did he know Eddie was dead, that he had been executed? There was a soft swish of rockets and a far-off shout. You're going to tell me, I said inwardly, addressing my absent father, you're going to tell me, after all these years, and I know already. Yes. All right. But why is my mother so upset? She knew. And she knew my father knew. He must have told her. What's so new and terrible in here? Now I know my father's secret, but what's my mother's? What has it to do with my father's? Grandfather lay back for a moment. He wasn't going to confess to any damn priest, he said. But he'd told my mother. And now he'd tell me. For she would never tell my father or me, and it had to be told. He wished he could tell my father the whole story. What story? I was standing, almost shouting at him. What story? He shut his eyes and he told me, told me. He, Grandfather, had ordered the execution. But he was wrong. Eddie had been set up. He had not been an informer at all. He told me who the real informer was.

I left him and went straight home, home, where I could never talk to my father or my mother properly again.

Two days later, Grandfather was taken to the hospital, semi-conscious, almost completely disabled by a stroke. He lay impervious to the world, to the visitations of the priest who did the daily rounds, to the visits of his children and grandchildren, to the nurses and doctors who were simply going through the motions, keeping him as comfortable as possible while everyone waited for the end. It came quickly. He died in his sleep. I saw him in the morgue, shrivelled inside his coffin like an ancient child, and then we all bore the whole routine again – the wake, the carrying of the coffin to the cathedral the night before the funeral, the requiem Mass (which I knew he would have scorned), the long traipse across the Lone Moor Road to the cemetery, the priests out ahead with their sashes slanted across them shoulder to waist, the women watching from the pavement, for they did not walk at funerals, the gravediggers with their stained spades, the prayers at the graveside, the tears, the wind slicing through us, the relief. I was sick with apprehension through it all, hoping that with his death the effect of what he had told me would magically pass away or reduce, even though I knew it could not but re-embed itself in my mother and go on living. We were pierced together by the same shaft. But she didn't know that. Nor was I going to say anything unless she did. And even then, when it had all been told, I had the sense of something still held back, something more than she knew, something Grandfather had cut out.

I pretended to my mother that I believed she was so upset just because of Grandfather's death and that I was encouraging her to talk to me about him – as I tried to do – so that she might feel better. It was easier when Aunt Katie came in, because she talked readily, even with a sense of liberation, about him. At first, they would go on and on like theologians, arguing that he must have received the grace to die in the faith, for the priest had blessed him and he died so peacefully. Other times, they would be upset to think that he had refused the Last Sacraments, that he went to eternity without having had his sins forgiven. At that thought, they would weep. 'Unforgiven, unforgiven,' they would cry. I would have a sudden sense of the scale of the lives these women lived as I watched them dab at their eyes, or sit with their hands over their faces, their shoes wrinkled and turned inward toward one another, in a circle. The dimensions of that other world opened around me and my stomach contracted. It was no use saying to myself that I believed none of this. There it was, a vast universe in which Grandfather's spirit moved lightless, for ever extinct, for ever alive to its own extinction, while his daughters mourned within the tiny globe of this kitchen and the world he had so austerely left. They would sit silent then, while the lids of the saucepans trembled on the range and the bubbling water gargled.

They also remembered Grandfather's weekend drinking binges that suddenly stopped. Katie remembered seeing him one Monday morning, standing at the sink, emptying a bottle of whiskey down the drain, his face averted as though he could not bear to watch. It was clear in her mind, she said, because that was the week, in July 1926, McIlhenny went to Chicago, leaving her pregnant with Maeve. When she said McIlhenny's name, just that, just his surname, she made a noise that sounded like a curse. My mother drooped her head and Katie just nodded at her, sympathetically, though it seemed to me that it was Katie who deserved the sympathy. Not a drop of alcohol, said Katie, passed her father's lips after that. Was it the Mahon trial, was it just before, just after that? Katie was eight years younger than my mother. She always deferred to her superior knowledge about the past. But my mother said no, it wasn't then, it wasn't even near then, it wasn't on account of that. Sure he stopped drinking several times, every two or three years. He stopped in 1921. Even before the Mahon trial. But he started again, maybe a year later. Maybe he had stopped for good in 1926. She couldn't remember now what the reasons were, why he stopped drinking so suddenly and then would just as suddenly start again. I stared at her and saw the lie spreading across her face like a change of expression. I knew what had stopped him drinking in 1922. It was after Eddie, and Eddie was after the Mahon trial. And in 1926, it was the discovery that McIlhenny was the informer, that Eddie had been innocent. She was turning the wedding band on her finger and looking at the floor. I hated having to love her

128

then, for it meant I couldn't say or ask anything, just go along with her, watch the gold ring shift back and forth on her finger, thinking, she's switching me off now, now she's switching me on; I want you to know now, I never want you to know, I never want you to want to know, I never want to know if you do know. The ring gleamed on and off. She put her right hand over her left and the ring disappeared under her strong fingers.

They went on talking about Grandfather. My father, God rest him, said Katie, was softer with me that time than he ever was before, than I could ever have imagined he could be. I suppose he felt sorry for me. God knows I felt sorry enough for myself, left pregnant like that. She stopped then and they sat in silence. But we've been through that often, she went on, and you don't want to hear any more of it. Though I wish to Christ I could understand why that man disappeared the way he did. My mother kept her face down. Her hair was greying. So Katie didn't know either. She looked at my mother for a moment, moving her top lip over the bottom one. She looked more than eight years younger. Her hair was still brown and curly, her skin was still fresh. She turned to me, smiling.

He wasn't much of a footballer himself, but he was a great organiser and he could see talent when others couldn't, she said. Football. Football. Katie wasn't interested in football. He said you could turn out a good wee player, she told me, smiling again. I nodded. The compliment was greater now that he was dead. He couldn't change his mind, or have it changed for him. He ran two clubs, Arsenal and Celtic Strollers, a red-and-white strip for one, green-and-white for the other. I fancied the red more but politically I was for the green. 'Get rid of the ball,' he would shout at me from the sideline. 'Cut the fancy stuff. Pass it.' But I would hold it until somebody up-ended me with a sweeping tackle and I would get up to see my father laughing and my grandfather glowering. Football was a dance, not a game. But Grandfather didn't think so. I couldn't have cared less. My mother was off the hook now on the question of when and why her father had stopped drinking. Did you do that on purpose? I asked Katie silently while smiling at her and recalling the weight of the full-back's tackles lifting me off the ground. One minute Grandfather's amiss in eternity, the next minute he's shouting from the sideline, my father huge beside him and my right leg is numb as I get up from the cindery pitch.

FATHER

February 1953

Out of the blue, Father suggested that Liam and I accompany him on a walk to Culmore Point and then take a rowboat across the river to where they were going to build the British Oxygen plant. It would be as well, he said, to have a stroll around there before the building work started, because that whole side of the embankment was going to disappear in a short while. We agreed. When we hired the rowboat, the sky was darkening, and a wind was whipping up, then dying away in strange half-shouted echoes that ricocheted along the banks down towards the estuary. He was strong but didn't row well, and the boat was soon slipping sideways on the glassy current, then straightening as the wind came streaking in, lifting us and the waves in buckling ups and downs. Rain and spray prickled our faces. He sat in the middle, and we were at either end. I pulled the straps of my leathery black helmet tighter under my chin and watched Liam rise up and disappear below my father's moving shoulders as we slipped and shuddered our way across. By the time we reached the opposite bank we were soaked, and the rain was coming down fast and serious. We took shelter under some trees for a while, but they soon began to shed their water loadings on us too, so we simply walked through the rain amidst the loud and glittering trees on the embankment path. He said little, just urged us on now and then as we cut inland towards Ardmore. The rain lifted away, the sunlight lay piebald on the path for a brief time, then the rain shuttered us in again. It was a dogged walk.

We finally took shelter in a country church that lay open on the curve of a road, separated thereby from its village. We sat in its tinted darkness, the rain dripping from us in clock-steady drops, watching the reds and greens on the one stained-glass window behind the altar go into depressions of their brightness as the sky outside darkened and small artilleries of thunder rattled in the distance. My father sat with his raincoat on the pew beside him, staring at the Sacred Heart lamp burning in its chained vessel above the altar: crimson, scarlet, crimson, steady, flickering, steady. Liam pulled off his helmet, and his red hair stood up in spikes on the crown of his head. He slashed the helmet sideways, and a scattering of water flew across the tiled floor. That pleased both of us, so I did the same. My father moved at that and suggested we sit down for a while and that we might even pray a little. 'Say a prayer for your mother,' he said. 'And one for me, while you're at it. It can do no harm.' He smiled mildly at that, so we both knelt down and made to pray, in awkwardly devotional attitudes. 'Oh, c'mon, don't make a meal of it,' he laughed, 'you can pray as well without trying to look like little saints.' We sat up, but I felt enormously shy. The little church was watchful, not sure of the strangers who had entered into its squat peace. We both giggled. He leaned across in amusement to look at us.

'What's so funny?' he asked.

We giggled the more.

'Pair of headcases, that's what ye are.'

But he was smiling broadly.

'This whole area, from here back to the river, is going to be industrialised,' he told us in a half-whisper. He had wanted us to see it because he had come here often as a child, with his parents, for his mother had had relatives in this part, although they were long gone now. They were well-off too, those relatives. Two servants and a pony and trap. He remembered his father and Eddie sitting up in the trap, his father holding the reins, and Eddie whistling to the horse to make it go. On another day, he remembered Eddie being lifted on to the horse's back, and how it paced round slowly at first with Eddie jogging on it; then Eddie dug his heels in, and the pony broke into a gallop across the greensward in front of the house, with his father and other grown-ups running after him and shouting. But Eddie kept on going, ducking his head as the horse went under a line of trees, whooping and waving his arm in the air. He was a wild one, Eddie.

Now, he said, he wished he could remember if this was the church they came to sometimes on a Sunday on those visits. He looked around as he said so, and so did we, as if some memory would return to us too. The saints in the stained glass looked mournfully down upon the altar, and a cherub strained upwards above gaping apostles towards a sunburst of Holy Ghost light. But he couldn't be sure. I knew this was his last visit here, as it was our first. I imagined the church bell ringing through the wet foliage outside, and my father as a small boy walking towards it, Eddie on a horse behind him, his parents sedately bringing up the rear of the small procession, the sea conquering the coastline beyond in wave after wave.

'Eddie was never killed in that shoot-out,' he said suddenly and looked away from us immediately.

He had said it, and I felt calm as death. Liam said nothing. The sentence disappeared into the church, then reappeared inside my head. We had to say something. Liam asked what happened then, if he wasn't killed? I could have embraced him for asking but I wanted to stop him too. For once, I knew more than he did. Than either of them did. It was like being a father to both of them, knowing more. I looked straight in my father's face, and it was hard to see him squint with the effort of telling us his heavy, untrue story. I wanted to touch his cheek with my hand to relax the muscle that appeared on it and touch the greying bristles that were visible in the curious light. His chin was down as though he were tucking a violin under it.

'No, he wasn't killed in the distillery. He was an informer. His own people killed him.'

Now he had said it all, and a great shame and sorrow was weighing his head down towards the front of the pew.

133

He wasn't looking at us. Raindrops scattered on the pale side windows and clip-clopped on the ground. I could see Eddie, plain as day, on horseback, one arm raised, the horse leaping with its head down, like a rodeo animal. I rubbed my hand on my wet face. I should stop this. Mother, I should stop this. You should stop this. Would it be worse? 'Daddy,' I said internally, 'I know it's too late but go back a few minutes, back into the church and the rain and say nothing. Never say. Never say.'

He was talking all the time, forcing it out of himself, and Liam's face was white as a star beside him. Informer. Betrayed his companions. Why he did it could not be known. His brother. Thank God his parents were not alive to see it. It was so stale a secret, like a gust of bad breath, and the way the three of us were crouched together in the middle pew of the church, like conspirators, with the sun beginning to shine, and the birds cheeping and warbling again, it was like a false relief, as though the church were a machine that had stopped throbbing to let the world come in again around its becalmed silence.

'Does Mother know?' Liam asked.

He nodded.

'Is that why she's been so upset? Did you just recently tell her?'

He shook his head. She had known since just after they were married. After? I wondered at that. How had her father felt when he heard whom she was going out with, whom she was going to marry? Did my grandmother know too? Would she not have done something? It should never have been allowed. It was worse than the breaking of the laws of consanguinity that we learned about in Christian doctrine class. It was a blood feud, more than the other one in my father's family. This was the real feud. The word had earned its keep at last. The farmhouse feud seemed ridiculous now. But not to him. Not unless I said something. Oh, Mother, what did your parents say when you told them you were going to marry Frank? The big gom, walking into it, innocent as a lamb, believing he had a dirty secret inside him, telling her after she was married to him. And did she know then, did she pretend she was hearing it for the first time? No. I couldn't believe that. I wished he had told her beforehand. It would have made him more innocent. I would have loved him even more. But I couldn't afford to love him any more than this, otherwise my face would start to break up into little patches and I would have to hold it together with the strap of my helmet. Please, Liam, ask no more questions.

He didn't. We sat there awhile. I knew my father had been praying a little but somehow I hadn't heard him. Liam's face was composed. He was feeling grown-up, I thought to myself. He can take this into himself better than I can, that's what he was thinking as I saw him look at me, and I knew I looked as thrown as he expected me to be.

My father sighed and got up to leave. Then it occurred to me.

'How did you know about Eddie? Who told you?' I asked, even though I wanted it all to be over. But it couldn't be over until he told me everything.

'I wondered when one of you was going to ask that. I knew eight months after it happened, from my sisters, Ena and Bernadette, when they got out of the farmhouse near Buncrana, where they'd been mistreated, and got up to Derry. They were there, in the farmhouse, the night after the fire. That's where they brought Eddie – or where Eddie brought them, that's where they interrogated him, that's where they took him away from to his death. They were the last to see him.'

He talked on about it, but, though I heard what he said, it seemed so obvious now, yet so incredible as well, that I could not absorb it, locate it there, at the farm, where it had happened, recognise what the farmhouse meant to him.

'So,' Liam asked, 'what were we doing there when we were small? What was that all about?'

It had to do with the aunt dying and leaving in her will

some possessions from his parents' home. He had gone to collect them, but to no avail. They would yield nothing.

He and Liam moved down the aisle, still talking. I was slow to follow them.

We went out into the sunshine and walked home. I stayed close alongside him the whole way, even though I knew that he too was believing – partly for the wrong reasons – that I was upset and clinging to him, walking in the lee of his hurt. When we came into the kitchen, my mother looked up and the whole history of his family and her family and ourselves passed over her face in one intuitive waltz of welcome and then of pain.

CHAPTER FOUR

CHAPTER FOUR

MOTHER

May 1953

My mother moved as though there were pounds of pressure bearing down on her; and when she sat, it was as though the pressure reversed itself and began to build up inside her and feint at her mouth or her hands, making them twitch. I knew now, or thought I knew, what it was, especially when I watched her eyes follow my father with such fear and pity that I wondered he didn't stop dead and realise there was something wrong, something she wanted to be forgiven for. I couldn't tell him if she didn't. I couldn't even let her know that I knew. It would make her more frightened, more depressed. I longed to find some way to give her release, but could think of nothing; every set of words that came to my mouth felt lethal. I would come in to find her at the turn of the stairs, looking out the lobby window, still haunted, but now with a real ghost crouched in the air around her. She would come down with me, her heart jackhammering, and her breath quick, to stand at the range and adjust the saucepans in which dinner simmered, her face in a rictus of crying, but without tears.

She was always on the stairs, usually at the lobby window, looking out, whispering to herself, sometimes crying out an incoherent noise. Once, when I came up, she turned to me, her eyes wet.

'Burning. It's burning. All out there, burning.'

She flapped her hand at the field beyond the window. Then she turned away again, her mouth working like a muscle in her still face.

It was always like that. Even at night, we would be wakened by voices and come downstairs to find her sobbing in the backyard, freezing in her nightdress, resisting my father's attempts to lead her back in.

'What is it, love?' he would ask.

'Burning; it's all burning,' she would cry, dragging her hand away from him and going a few steps away, her arms clasped round herself, staring towards the sky.

'Come to bed; you'll get your death of cold; c'mon now, there's a love.'

But she would shake her head and keep staring beyond, her face shiny with tears.

Everyone would be awake, huddled at the back door, watching them both in the yard: he with his raincoat over his pyjamas, she slippery in the light and dark, moving always towards the blackness beyond the range of the kitchen light. Then, always, when he reached her down there near the yard wall, there was a murmuring and a sobbing, and his arm would black out her shoulders as it went round her. And they would come up towards us, she with her head bent, all of us retreating into the kitchen, out to the foot of the stairs in the hall, as he led her to the fold-out bed and persuaded her to lie down. I could see her shiver as the blankets were drawn over her and he came to shoo us up the stairs to bed, his face heavy and graven, the stubble visible on his cheeks.

'What does she mean?' I would ask him. 'What's burning? What's the matter with her?'

'It's a kind of sleepwalking,' he would say, 'dreaming. She's upset; but don't worry, she'll come round and be all right.'

'What's got her upset?'

'It's losing her father. And it's brought Una — losing Una — back in on her too.'

We were all frightened. Also, I was ashamed. When I saw her wandering around the house, touching the walls, tracing out the scrolls of varnish on the sitting-room door with her finger, or climbing wearily up the stairs to gaze out of the window, my cheeks burnt and the semi-darkness seemed to be full of eyes. She was going out from us, becoming strange, becoming possessed, and I didn't want anyone else outside the family to know or notice.

Besides, I always had the feeling that there was someone else who had died, someone besides' Una, or my mother's father or mother, or Eddie, someone I knew of, someone secret for whom hope had long been lost. And it had something to do with my father. Something made worse by his having told us about Eddie being an informer. I could understand, but only in part. There was something missing. My mother's grieving was so inconsolable, I thought it must be for a lost soul, someone woven into the fires of hell the way gas was into a flame. I used to sit beside her at the grate and watch the coal burn. After a piece started to smoke heavily, there would be the tiniest hiss as the flame took. She would see me watching.

'See that?' she'd say. 'The pain is terrible. The flame is you, and you are the flame. But there's still a difference. That's the pain. Burning.'

Then she would weep again. Sometimes she'd let me hold her hand as she cried. Sometimes she'd brush my hand away and sit rigid, with only the tears moving on her face until she was wet under the chin and the skin in the valley of her throat looked liquid.

The doctor came and gave her pills and medicines. She'd take them and become calmer, but her grief just collected under the drugs like a thrombosis. When it took over, overcoming the drugs, her body shook and her eyes glimmered with tears that rarely flowed but shone there, dammed up in her tear-ducts, dangerous. She was in such pain she could not cry, only wish that she could. I could touch her, run my finger over the curve of her forearm, rub my thumb against the inside of her wrist with its thick blue vein, and she would seem to feel nothing. 'This is my mother,' I would say to myself. 'This is my mother.' I dreamt of a magic syringe that I could push up into the inside skin of her arm and withdraw, black with grief, and keep plunging it and withdrawing it, over and over, until it came out clear, and I would look up in her face and see her smiling and see her eyes full of that merriment I thought I remembered. Her hair was cold. Her skin was stretched glossy on her bones and tightening with wrinkles. 'Oh, Jesus,' my father would say under his breath, the holy name hissing in his mouth like snakes in a pit, 'Oh, Jesus, Jesus, where have you gone, love?' He tilted her chin very gently to lift her face to the evening light, and she would respond with the tiniest of uninterested smiles. As he withdrew his hand, and she lowered her face again, I thought – he thought – that she said, 'Burning, burning,' but it was really only a noise she made, and all her noises had come to sound in our ears like that word, and when my father sigh-heaved himself out of the chair, making my nose sting with all the salty, chalky smells of the docks that were folded into the wrinkles of his dungarees, he too sounded as if he were saying that word even though his voice was just a hum in his throat. I'd put my hands down inside my socks, as far as my ankles, and grip the bones and tighten myself up for a while before I could walk away from her tilted face and her quietly folded hands and the troubling chill of her black-grey hair.

Liam and I played football in the backyard, our movements quick and loud with the panic we both felt. If we fought, we did so in the same high-edged way, striking clean blows, no wrestling or snarling about. The sky sloped up into the sun and down into the stars, and she went on, scarcely moving, haunted and burning, audibly, inaudibly.

Then, at last, the real crying began, a lethal sobbing that ran its fright through us like an epidemic. Sundays were the worst. We'd come back from Mass, all spruced up, my sisters fresh and ingeminated in their light-green tweed coats, my brothers and I self-conscious in shirts and ties, with our hair sticking up at odd angles because of Liam's advice that we should soak it in a mix of sugar and water 'to make it sit still'.

Father was a stride before us as we went into the hall, for he could hear her sobbing, a sound that moved and wavered in phases, a stripping-off of unbearably tight panics that only found more – tighter ones – within. I wanted to run away, to flee across Meenan's Park past the Sunday football games, past the crouching players of marbles, and the children on swings with their legs out stiff, past the card-players squatting on the broken slabs of the air-raid shelters in a pale blue trance of smoke, and on into the shuttered Lecky Road, up the long hill to Bishop Street, down Abercorn Road to the river and over the bridge into the safety of really foreign territory, the estrangement of Protestants with their bibles and the ache of the railway line curving away towards Coleraine, Portstewart, Belfast. But I also wanted to run into the maw of the sobbing, to throw my arms wide to receive it, to shout into it, to make it come at me in words, words, words and no more of this ceaseless noise, its animality, its broken inflection of my mother. Instead, I stood there and looked at her while my father pottered helplessly about her and everyone came over and touched her, petted her, stroked her hair, let tears roll on their cheeks. Eilis knelt in front of her and squeezed her, face against her stomach, but my mother's arms hung helplessly down by her sides, and her semi-brushed hair fell sideways across her streaming face. The hairbrush lay in the corner of the kitchen where she must have thrown it. I picked it up and tugged at the strands of her hair caught in the wire bristles, winding them round my fingers, feeling them soften on my skin as though the tightness were easing off them into me. I felt it travelling inside, looking for a resting place, a nest to live in and flourish, finding it in the cat's cradle of my stomach and accumulating there.

She cried for weeks, then months. A summer passed in a nausea of light, and we took turns at the cooking and shopping, we all did odd jobs for extra shillings round the area – collecting scrap metal, rags, jamjars, and selling them to a dealer on the Lecky Road. His shed was always dark, mounded with piles of the stuff. In the yard behind, a cart always sat with its shafts in the air, their tips catching light. Everything else was mauve dark, and all the smells of the place came with him as he approached to look at what we had brought. He wore a begrimed raincoat, belted, with its collar turned up in all weathers. His hair was wild and wiry, his trousers ragged; but his shoes were always clean. When he gave us the coins, they chinked into our hands but they had no brightness, so dirty were they. We would wash them in suds at the sink and feel we had revealed their true value when they came up glistening brown, yellow, silver. I always felt better-paid when I put the clean coins on the mantel-piece, or showed them to my mother. She sometimes took them and put them in her apron pocket and said, 'That's grand. You're good children. Good wee'uns.' But when one of us would ask her later for the money to buy food, she would look puzzled, and we would have to fish them out of her pocket and show them to her. That often made her weep again. I was glad when the darker weather came again. It was more appropriate, especially when the wind drove the rain at a sharp slant into me as I ran from the grocer's with a stone of potatoes, carrots, onions and a round of country butter, heavy with salt, bumping against my legs in the cloth shopping-bag. When the snow came, I fractured my arm in a spill from a sleigh that crashed into the wall at the end of the street. My mother would ask me to take the clumsy plaster-of-Paris casing out of the sling and she would caress it as though she could reach the arm inside. It felt strange to hear and see her hand move on the plaster and not feel anything except its light pressure and an itch writhing in ringworm patterns inside.

'Paradise was not far away when I died,' she said one day – a Tuesday in February – into clear air, when my father was washing the dishes, and Deirdre and I were drying and putting them away. It made me smile, that remark. The blue willow-pattern plate I was holding was light and burnished as I stacked it on the shelf. I knew for the first time, in a real way, that she had been in love. Her voice was clear and young; sure enough, when I stepped into the kitchen from the scullery to look at her, she was smiling to herself. I looked towards my father, but he was staring into the sudsy water, his thick arms plunged in and still. Deirdre batted her eyelids at me, signalling her own amusement. Then, some weeks later, one Friday in April, when Mother was folding sheets at the ironing-board, she said in the same voice, 'Not far. I could see the rim of it.' This was her new conversation. Connected remarks separated by days, weeks, months, but always in her new voice. I knew she was getting stranger; she was telling herself a story that only appeared now and again in her speech.

She talked mostly to the younger children, Gerard, Eamon, Deirdre. Sometimes she would hold Gerard's little round flaxen head close to her breast and bend down to say things in her new voice into his shy face, things that enthralled and mystified me. 'To go halfway round the globe and never speak again. The poor coward. The lonely soul.' I listened, envying him. I had the impression she was talking to him and to the others in little confidential bursts, but was leaving my father, Eilis, Liam and me out of it. Once, when I had taken the back off the wireless and was trying to get it to work again, she leaned over and clicked her fingernail against one of the valves. It gave a hoarse ping and lit briefly before fading. A remark hung in the air between us, expanding in a bubble of light, but she said nothing. I left the wireless's entrails scattered on the table and took a rubber ball from the drawer. Since my arm fracture, I had been told to rebuild the wasted muscles by squeezing this ball, in, out, in, out, as often as possible. I stood there squeezing it and looking at her until my forearm was tired. She talked about this and that, evasively. How cruel she was! I longed for her to talk in her new voice to me, and she felt my longing and she resisted it. I went upstairs and sat on the bed in the cold bedroom and looked at the picture of the Sacred Heart and thought I understood how Jesus felt, him with his breast open and the pierced blood-dripping muscle emblazoned there. I still had the ball in my hand. I lobbed it against the glass of the picture, scoring a bull's-eye on the heart, and caught it on the first bounce. Her voice came up to me, young and clear in its inflection, but I didn't catch the words. I lay on the bed and wept. She had been in love with someone else, not quite my father. That's what she was telling, and not telling, him. And she was telling me. Most of all, she was telling herself. A great lamentation of seagulls filled the air as a storm came up from the harbour and the room seemed to lift into the sky with their rising shadows.

One day, it must have been the following winter, she went to the shelf where the round white boxes of pills were kept, and brought them in the lap of her apron over to me. She asked me to open the boxes and empty them out on to a saucer. I did. Then, she asked me to throw them into the fire. I did that too. They lay there in coloured specks, darkening into nothing. Then she brought out five medicine bottles, red, blue, yellow, two of them clear. She took a jug from the press and emptied them all in, one on top of the other. She asked me to smell it. I bent over and inhaled.

'Slime,' she said, nodding at me. 'Chemical slime. Putrid. It makes me sick. Sick even to think I ever took it. Look what it did to my teeth.' She showed me how her teeth had rotted. Then she went out to the scullery and poured it all down the sink. She came in and smiled at me, but her white smile was ruined now, had been for some time, and her breath was bad.

'I'm better now, son. But I'll never be as I was. You poor child. My poor family.'

She hugged my head to her breast. She still smelt of medicine and I could feel her older, as though her breath were shallower than it had once been. I held her for a

146

moment, ashamed of the shame I had been feeling. But I never felt less like asking anything. That night, for the first time in weeks, she made dinner and even talked about Hallowe'en and Christmas. By All Souls' Night, she had false teeth, and her smile was white again. But when I saw her smile, then and ever afterwards, I could hear her voice, creased with sorrow, saying, 'Burning, burning,' and I would look for the other voice, young and clear, lying in its crypt behind it. But it slept there and remained sleeping, behind her false white smile.

Her startling illness aged them both. My father's physical strength was still immense, but I sensed that he now began to feel it useless. Sometimes, when he came up the back lane from work, two or three of us would be standing on the backyard wall. As he came alongside, we would jump towards him. He would catch us one by one and swing us on to his shoulders, duck through the gate and then plant us back on the wall as though we weighed nothing. But once, after my mother's illness was over, when we jumped, he caught us – Eilis first, then Deirdre, then Gerard, then Eamon – but before Liam or I could jump, he let them slither gently down to the ground and waved us off.

'Not tonight, children. You're too many for me.'

I watched him go up the yard, leaving a trail of children behind him, and held tight to the clothes-line post as I teetered on the rounded wall-top. Liam was standing on his hands on the wall beside me, trying to keep his legs straight.

'He's far shook, that man, far shook,' he said upside-down. I remember thinking how strange his mouth was when he spoke in that position. Then he somersaulted off into the lane, landing on his feet. 'As you'd expect,' he added.

I nodded, but I hadn't expected it at all, not this fast, at least not until he said it. I slid off the wall carefully, as though from a great height, and felt grateful for the solidity

147

of the black loam of the lane under my boots. But even that solidity weakened as I moved to the gate and saw, through the kitchen window, her smiling her false teeth at him as they talked.

THE FACTS OF LIFE

September 1953

The school's Spiritual Director wanted to see me. My name was called out in class. I was summoned to go to Father Nugent's room. Everyone smiled knowingly. This was the facts-of-life talk we were all individually given. The near-albino, Nigger Crossan, squeezed the inside of my thigh as I edged out of the desk past him. He had told us things that made the head swim. Father Nugent had never called him in. This was taken to be a compliment to Nigger's superior knowledge, or an insult to his irredeemable depravity.

Although it was a warm day, Nugent had a fire blazing and an armchair drawn close up on either side. He was a small man with grizzled hair, rimless spectacles and a shiny innocent face. He rarely raised his voice, rarely lost his temper and had never been known to strike anyone. He asked if I minded if he smoked. I shook my head. He cast around looking for matches, then said it was bad for him anyway.

'You could light it from the fire, Father,' I said.

'Of course, you're right, you're right there. Very good.'

He lit the cigarette with a spill of paper, dropped himself into the armchair opposite me and nodded at me through the blue spiral of smoke. Then he switched on the lamp on the table beside him, even though it was a bright day. I was toasting on the side nearest the fire, so I moved the chair back as unobtrusively as I could by levering my heels gently against the thin carpet. The carpet rucked behind the chair. I was stuck. As he stared into the fire, brooding in a kind-hearted and embarrassed manner before the red coals, I rehearsed the sequence that others had told me to expect. First, the life-is-a-mystery bit. Then, the incarnation – spirit becoming flesh. Reference to Jesus. To His Mother. None to Joseph. Then to Our Own Parents, Adam and Eve. Then to the Fall. Then to our own parents at home. Then to it, the act itself.

He did as I had been told he would. You were born, he told me – after the early parts were over – of your parents. This I knew, but didn't think it mannerly to say so in any raucous fashion. As a result, he continued, of the act of sexual intercourse between your parents. I knew this too, but here my curiosity did light up, for I didn't know, although I had heard much, what this was. What I had heard was certainly improbable. It sounded like a feat of precision engineering, one I could never quite associate with what the Church called lust, which seemed wild, fierce, devil-may-care, like eating and drinking together while dancing to music on top of the table. I knew, but did not know. I wanted to know, but did not want to find out that I already knew. I wanted to know something different, a subtler way of being with a woman, as he called it, although I disliked the vagueness of that. Most of all, I wanted to believe it was different for my parents and for that whole generation before us; so that this sexual intercourse, if it were true, would be for us only, our generation's problem, and there'd be no embarrassment involved in looking at them afterwards.

'. . . came together in love,' he was saying. I nodded appreciatively, although so far, I realised with panic, I had heard almost nothing. I decided to attend, but he chose that moment to stir the fire with a long-handled poker and we both watched the coals heave up their red sides and sparkle. I thought of the girl I fancied, Irene Mackey. I could come together with her all right if I could only get up the nerve to speak to her. Father Nugent was talking about passion. Love breeds passion. In passion, the body alters. The penis . . . Had I heard that word before? Did I know it? I knew it, but I'd never heard it. I nodded vigorously. Penis? So that's what they called it.

'Yes.'

A moment later, he said 'vagina' and was asking me if

I knew that word, and what it was. I knew what it must be but I couldn't envisage it and when he asked me if I knew where it was, I gave a slightly hysterical smile and said yes, yes, I did, but I was telling myself, no, you don't, not really, ask him, you stupid shit, ask him, that's what you're here for, but I couldn't do anything except stare at him and feel my head nodding every so often although I didn't know at what, for all I could see were his lips moving back and forth, up and down, and his teeth appearing and disappearing and the firelight glinting in his glasses at times so that his eyes seemed balefully red, and his black soutane gave him the appearance of a strange animal with burning eyes that was leaning forward, purring, to spring.

'When the enlarged penis enters the vagina, seed is emitted.'

Emitted? Holy Christ, emitted? He-mit-it? He-mid-it? What word was that? I forced my voice out.

'He what?'

Father Nugent paused, eyebrows raised. 'He . . . ?'

Then he caught on.

'Oh, emitted. From the Latin, *emittere*, to send out. The seed is sent out.'

This puzzled me. It seemed a very distant procedure.

'You mean he sends it to her?' In what? I wanted to ask. An envelope? In a wee parcel? What, in the name of Christ, was this nutcase talking about?

'In a sense. The more technical word is "ejaculated".'

Oh, from the Latin, I knew he would say, as he did. Thank you, father. Now he's throwing it out, like a spear. And semen is the Latin for seed. Do you have to know Latin to do this? Does He say to Her, 'Here you are. This is from the Latin for throw or send'? If there's no Latin involved, that's what makes it a sin. Love is in Latin, lust isn't. I thought of all the words in English I had heard. They surely sounded a lot more savage.

'Do you understand now?' He was looking so sweetly at me that I hadn't the heart to say no, I was so totally

151

confused and I didn't know what the famous act was or how on earth my parents could have performed it without a good grounding in Latin roots. Maybe the sacrament of marriage gave you that knowledge, spontaneously, then you could do it the way the Church recommended. I brightened at that thought and he mistook my expression for illumination.

'You see, now?'

'Yes, Father.'

The seed grew into a child in the womb. Womb I knew from the Hail Mary, in Latin and in English. And in Irish. This was all pretty legit. I felt singed all down one side, and there was sweat gathering behind my right knee. He was looking at me questioningly. He must have asked me something. I changed my expression to try to look quizzical, raising my eyebrows and widening my eyes.

'Do you?'

Bereaved Christ's mother, do I what? What do I do? Should I pretend to faint from the heat? Would someone not knock at the door? In total gratitude, I heard him go on before I could get my tongue off the roof of my mouth.

'Most boys don't think of it at this age.'

You're wrong there, I shouted inside. A lot of them think of nothing else. But you're right about me. I'm normal.

'It's only later they ask themselves how an old celibate like me can know these things.'

That set me aslant. I thought he was talking about sex. Who cared if he was celibate? Celibacy was just a funny smell of soap and power. So, he went on, when I did come to think about this later – although I wanted to tell him nothing was less likely – but when I did, I would appreciate that there was a way of dedicating your life to a person, and a way of dedicating your life to God and that they were very similar for they were both founded on a love that was unconditional. He paused. I had heard that word before, on the day Liam and I had made our Confirmation. With Confirmation, the dread was being picked out of the crowd for questioning, sitting there in the church, rows of us, while the Bishop walked up the aisle escorted by two priests and an altar boy walking behind him, holding the hem of his robe. Every so often he would stop on his way to the altar, look across a row and point to someone. That boy would then be ushered out and had to stand waiting at the end of the row with one of the teachers until the Bishop reached the altar, sat down on his throne, spread his vestments wide and beckoned for the boys to be brought up. We all slumped down as tight as we could and stared at the floor. He stopped at the end of our row. I sensed him scanning us and sensed his fat little finger pointing. 'It's you,' whispered Liam, 'he's pointing at you.' I saw the finger pointing and the teacher starting to work his way along the row. He placed his hand on my shoulder. 'Not me, Sir. It's Campbell he was pointing at.' Busty Campbell, beside me, dug his elbow into my ribs. 'No, sonny,' said the teacher, 'it's you. Don't be nervous. It'll be all right.'

Five of us were led up to the altar. We would be confirmed first, as soldiers of Christ, as members of the Church Militant on earth. He would touch our cheeks to symbolise the blows we would receive in defence of our faith and then he would confirm us by making the sign of the cross on our brows. But first, this random selection was to make sure the class had been taught the doctrines of the Church properly. Each knelt in front of the Bishop, he leaned over and asked questions, the pupil answered, was confirmed and led away to the side chapel where he would wait, in full view of the adults assembled along the side pews, to rejoin his row as it came up and returned. I was the last of the five.

The altar was sweet with incense. The gold-embroidered robe of the Bishop and his golden staff, held upright in his right hand, shone on me. I had the sensation that if he touched me I too would turn to gold, my face metalled and my legs heavy, my body precious and dead. The Bishop smiled at me.

'Tell me, my child, what is the central mystery of our faith?'

'The Incarnation of Christ, Your Lordship.'

That was easy. We had recited that endlessly in class.

'What does Incarnation mean? Can you tell me that?'

'The taking on of human flesh. God becoming Man.'

'Excellent.'

Father Browne, with his grey bushy hair, was nodding encouragement from behind the throne. The Bishop's plump hand moved towards me. I wanted to giggle, feeling my stomach move at the thought of his touch, at the thought it was all over. My face twitched and his hand stopped.

'One last question. What is the nature of God's love for mankind?'

I looked at his robe. No word came to me. My stomach started to grow a cold spot in its centre. He gazed at me. Father Browne had stopped nodding. Father Mullan, on the other side of the throne, was frowning at me. The crowded cathedral behind me was almost perfectly silent, although someone coughed. Heat from the congregation reached me and passed through me, leaving me wet. I thought of crying, but then thought I should answer the question somehow. Then I realised I had forgotten it. What had he asked? It came back to me.

'Unconditional,' I whispered.

Everyone smiled. The Bishop struck my cheek a light blow, rubbed his thumb on my brow, muttered in Latin.

I knelt on. Father Browne signalled with his hand that I was to get up. I knelt there, ensnared.

'Unconditional,' I said again.

The Bishop leaned over and said,

'You can get up now. Your teacher will take you over.'

But I could not move. I *had* become golden. My whole body was solid: an ingot. They would have to lift me and carry me off the altar and put me kneeling in a niche in the wall of the side chapel. Father Browne touched my shoulder, and I rose at once, the teacher caught my elbow and escorted me to the side where the other four were standing and left me there with them, my skin crawling on my scalp and the word 'unconditional' running in my head, over and over, a word that shone on and off like a lighthouse beam out of my mouth and across the faces of the staring congregation, drowning in the sea of sound as the choir sang. That was the first time the Bishop spoke to me.

Nugent was still talking.

He had renounced the flesh for the sake of the spirit, he was saying. The flesh was good, good *in* itself but not *by* itself. That was an important distinction.

I agreed, nodding vigorously.

The danger of the flesh was, he announced, that it could become an appetite that lived by what it fed on.

He sat back and looked at me expectantly.

How else could something live? I wondered, but again he was smiling expectantly at me, and again I realised he had asked a question I had not heard. The noise in my head was deafening.

'You know that phrase – about appetite?' asked Father Nugent.

I looked at him, appalled. Was this something I was supposed to know?

'It's Shakespeare, I believe. One of the plays.'

The *plays*. I had thought there was only the one, *The Merchant of Venice*, which we were reading and rehearsing in third year. This man was ready for the asylum. Soon I would be too.

He leaned forward, and I sat back as far as I could go. The fire was windowed in his glasses.

'Sex without love is akin to murder. You are a murderer of your own body and of the body of the woman with whom you perform the loveless act. And in murdering the flesh, you murder also the soul.'

He leaned back, and the fires in his spectacles disappeared. I liked the way he had placed that 'also'. That was neat, truly official. He was going on.

'. . . the misuse of our most mysterious power, the power of originating life itself. Nothing else compares with it except the love from which that life springs, which is in God, and the love that life brings forth in us – that too is in God, of course, but is also what moulds, defines and sanctifies us all our days.'

He paused and took breath. I was nodding again but I was beginning to make the smallest possible definite movements in the chair to signal that I thought the show was over.

'One thing. When it comes to women. Above all things. Avoid brutality. That will make a man of you. Not strength. Not fighting. Not sport. Not money. A lot of your companions are . . . what shall I say? A little raucous, you know? Tough for the sake of being tough, you know what I mean, son? Avoid that. Go in peace.'

He stood up and blessed me with a swift sign of the cross that pinned me back in the chair for a moment. He left me to the end of the corridor with its lines of green baize doors on either side. I ran from the building, cut out the back gate to intercept Irene Mackey, if I could, on the way home from her school for lunch. Just to look at her and persuade myself she was looking at me. As I ran, I imagined Father Nugent hesitantly closing his door and looking at the armchairs on either side of the fire, now mute and emptied of all confidences in the whitened light of his lamp and the tall windows.

GOING TO THE PICTURES

November 1953

We saw the movie *Beau Geste*. The idea of lodging the corpses of the dead legionnaires on the parapets seemed to us ingenious, although there was a great deal of argument about how dead men could stand so with a rifle tucked under their arms, and how the Tuareg tribesmen could have failed to notice.

We took up the evil sergeant's announcement as a slogan that we chanted regularly when we walked in a group through the Protestant area that lay between the school and our streets.

'Everybody does his duty at Zinderneuf, dead or alive. We'll make the Arabs think we've got a thousand men.'

The history teacher rebuked us for admiring all that English public-schoolboy nonsense in the movie. The three brothers. The stolen jewel. The so-called Viking funeral at the end for the dead Beau. The name Beau Geste itself. We should learn more about the Irish tradition in the French Foreign Legion. For instance, the great Fenian organiser, John Devoy, had joined the Legion in his youth in order to get the military training for fighting the English. The French were always our friends, he said.

So they say, so they say, my father told me. But really, it's just a case of one empire or another. France and America were republics; they should never have gone on to become empires. Real republicans would never do that. But then, he asked, with a marked bitterness, who ever met a real republican? Rarer than a real Christian. He lifted the newspaper in front of his face again.

Your brother, you met him, I wanted to say. Your own brother. He was one. But you'll never know it. Instead I asked him why Devoy had joined up with the French to fight Arabs so that he could then fight for Ireland against the British Empire. He shrugged his shoulders. Maybe he saw too many movies, he laughed.

But every other Saturday afternoon, when the football team did not have a home game, we went to the pictures in the City Cinema or in St Columb's Hall. Once, on a feast day, when there was no school, we went to a six o'clock showing. Irene Mackey had finally agreed to go with me and the others on this occasion. She was still Grenaghan's girlfriend; the presence of the others made her feel it was safe enough to come with me. He was a tough, even though he walked with a limp. But I'd worry about him later, I decided. She'd be sitting beside me. That was enough. To my right was Harkin and Moran. To Irene's left was Toner, his girlfriend, Sheila, and then O'Donnell. With everyone else we jeered at the advertisements and a documentary about growing wheat on the Canadian plains. Then the real movie – a thriller – began. I inched closer to Irene, and she snuggled in towards me. Someone behind kicked the back of my chair and laughed.

'You two behave yourselves,' said a man's voice.

We both blushed and parted slightly. Harkin, who was eating from a tub of ice-cream, whispered to me:

'Just say the word an' I'll turn round and fix your man behind. One smack in the gob.'

Irene looked at me in horror.

'No. Forget it. We'll watch the movie.'

After a time, as the plot unravelled, O'Donnell began to lay bets on what would happen, and who the murderer was.

'Who's the fucker in the bedroom? A tanner says it's the da, the big fella with the glasses.'

'Her da? Never. Let's see your tanner and you're on,' whispered Harkin across Irene and me. O'Donnell's hand came out of the gloom with a silver sixpence in the palm. Then it withdrew.

'You're on,' said Harkin, displaying his own tanner.

We were all slumped back, caught in the glare of the screen above us. The film's heroine went into the kitchen and made coffee.

'Is coffee much different from tea?' whispered Sheila.

'Don't be stupid,' answered Toner in embarrassment, 'it's away different.'

'How do you know?' cackled O'Donnell from the other side. 'You never drank coffee in your life.'

'I did so. Out at the American base one day. I was out there delivering stuff from Lipton's shop, and they gave me coffee then. Plenty o' times, so I did.'

'Be quiet, you lot,' said the man's voice from behind us, 'some people want to hear the picture. That's what we paid money for.'

The usherette's torch danced over us, and we slid down a little in the seats. Everybody shushed. The picture had reached its crisis. A detective on the screen was questioning a suspect.

Moran, craned across, whispering: 'Did you hear the joke about the Eskimo detective? He said to the suspect, "Where were you on the night of the twenty-first of September to the twenty-first of March?" '

Toner laughed out loud.

'I don't get it,' said Sheila.

'Never mind; we'll tell you after. Jesus.'

'What's the joke?' whispered Irene in my ear.

'He didn't tell it right. I'll tell you outside.' A pang crossed my stomach. She didn't get *that*?

On the screen, a door handle turned and the door edged open into the hallway. There was a glimpse of a gloved hand.

Nat was leaving. The door opened further.

'Eedjit,' roared Moran, 'your man's in the bedroom. Keep bonehead talking.'

'Shhh,' said the man behind.

A girl was sobbing some rows back.

'She's going to be killed. Why doesn't someone tell her?'

'Hi, Miss, you're going to be killed,' shouted Harkin.

Some people laughed, but there was much shushing too, and the usherette's light played across us and stayed for a few seconds. Irene gripped my hand tightly. I twisted mine round hers, and we interwove our fingers.

On screen, the hero was at the door, preparing to leave.

'NO, NO, NO,' we roared in unison. 'You gom. You're lockin' her in with him. He's in the bedroom.'

'She's had it now,' Toner announced.

Sheila began to weep. Irene clung to my arm.

'I can't look,' she whispered. 'Tell me when it's all over.'

'But this is the best bit!'

But she dug her face in my shoulder and wouldn't look. The cinema was silent.

'Jesus, it *is* her da,' whispered Toner, as the camera settled on a photograph of the heroine's father.

'You owe me a tanner, Harkin,' said O'Donnell gleefully, banging his hands together.

The killer pulled the mask from his face. It *was* her father. I was horrified. I forgot Irene.

'Her da?' squealed Sheila in disbelief. 'He wouldn't kill his own daughter.' 'ANIMAL!' she roared at the screen. The people around us laughed.

The hero was pounding his way up the stairs, gun drawn.

A shot, an embrace, a voice-over. *The End*.

'Jesus, that was good,' said Toner as the lights went up, 'I knew it was him all the time.'

'On your arse, you did,' jeered Moran, 'you thought it was the man in the drugstore. Anyone would've known it was the da.'

I left Irene to my own street corner, since she thought we

might be more likely to meet Grenaghan at her own. We stood near the street lamp. I could see my own door from there and I kept an eye on it in case anyone came out to leave out the milk bottles for the morning. We kissed once, very softly. As I leant forward to kiss her again, I wondered if I could suggest we get out of the light and go round to the back lane. A shadow came up on the wall above us, and I knew, even as she stepped away, that it was Grenaghan. He was just a blur moving close. The house door opened. My father stepped out in the block of yellow light. I saw him perfectly. Grenaghan stopped and looked. My father looked across at us. Then he stepped in again, leaving the door open. Grenaghan swung at me and caught me on the side of the head. Then Liam appeared with some of the others, including Harkin, Moran and O'Donnell. They all ran at Grenaghan who turned, leapt on the wall and dropped into the field below. They didn't follow him into the darkness.

Liam sat me against the wall.

'Where's Irene?' I asked.

'Irene? You're asking about her? She passed us a hundred yards down the road, running. Said nothing. She must have set you up for Grenaghan.'

I shook my head. It wasn't true. They all took me for a fool. But Irene avoided me thereafter, and I could not bring myself to pursue her and ask her outright. She stayed with Grenaghan. My father pulled down my lip to check the bruising on the inside.

'Standing in the light with your back to the dark. That's asking for it. You should have been on your guard. Anyway, you're too young to be running around with girls. Stick to your studies. And stay away from Grenaghan and anybody associated with him. You hear?'

He went out then and bolted the hall door before we went to bed. The house felt tight and small, and my head felt thunderous.

HAUNTED

December 1953

The story ran like this, said Liam, as he explained to me
why Grenaghan should be left alone. You've heard it before,
he told me, the old yarn about the diocesan exorcist, Father
Browne, whose hair went white in one night fighting
the devil. Christ knows what the devil looked like after a
night with that maniac. Anyway, it was that family – the
Grenaghans – it was all about. Years and years ago, Jimmy
Grenaghan, your man's grandfather, had been in love with a
woman called Claire Falkener. But he had been one of those
hopelessly shy men and had never told her, even though she
knew it. Everything was so strict then, at the turn of the
century. She couldn't say anything directly and he blushed
at the thought of addressing her or any woman. 'Better to
have loved and not be able to talk than ever to have talked
at all,' Liam cackled.

Claire waited and waited. Grenaghan watched her, but
said nothing. The Falkener family gave no encouragement.
Jimmy was never going to grow up. He walked in fear of
his own shadow and his smile, they said, was a smile at
nothing; it was just an apology for being in the world. And
anyway, who wanted a cringer like that in the family? So, in
the heel of the hunt, Claire tired of waiting, was courted by
another man, Danno Bredin, and married him. Bredin was
in the Merchant Navy, so he was away a lot, sometimes as
much as eight months in the year. They had three children, a
boy and two girls. To everybody's surprise, Jimmy Grenaghan
went off to England, looking for work. Nobody thought he
could ever get up the nerve to buy a ticket and leave his
mammy. But he did, and he stayed away for several years.
On top of all that, he came back to Derry as a qualified

tradesman and found a job in the local foundry. He was a different man by then, a changed person – no longer the shy stick he had been. He even looked different, walked different, dressed well, talked with confidence. England had transformed him, done him a world of good. But he never looked at another woman. Instead, he took to visiting Claire, becoming a kind of second father to the children, buying them presents, even going so far as to go out with her now and then to the New Year's pantomime, or out the country roads for a walk. People pulled in their breaths and hissed their gossip. But then, during the War, it was reported that Danno Bredin's ship had gone down off the coast of Argentina, all hands lost. Claire and Jimmy waited six months, then he moved into the house with her. They didn't marry; just lived together. The priest came down and gave off yards to her. She just listened and shut the door after him. When the priest came back, Jimmy met him and put his arm across the doorway and wouldn't let him in. Told him it was none of his business. A lot of the neighbours didn't speak to them. Jimmy was ostracised; so was Claire. It was worse for her, living in the street all day long. He, at least, had his work to go to as foreman of the foundry. So not many could turn a word in his mouth there. Then Danno Bredin returned. He had been injured in the shipping disaster and had a permanent limp and looked sick. He had been pensioned off. But there he was, limp and all, and the cuckoo, Jimmy, was in the nest.

Claire and Jimmy must really have been in love, for she wouldn't have Bredin around the place. Told him marriage to him was no marriage, with him away most of the time. Claimed he had relations with other women, she knew it for a fact. There was total uproar. Bredin could have gone to law for the house. But instead, he rented a bedroom in the house opposite them, that belonged to a widow, and sat in it, day after day, at the window, looking at his own house, his own children, across the way. He spoke to no one. He never went out, just sat there, a face at the window, looking

at what had become of his life. The street – Wellington
Street it was – had an uneasy air about it. People didn't like
passing between those two houses – even Claire, who started
to leave the house by the back, down the lane and on to the
Lecky Road so that she wouldn't see the shrivelling face of
her husband watching her. Jimmy ignored him, even made
a point of it by standing in the doorway smoking a cigarette
after dinner and looking up and down the street, letting
Bredin see he could not care less. Finally, one day, Bredin
was no longer at the window. He had become ill. He lingered
for a while. The doctor said there was no hope for him.
And sure enough, he died. The funeral was a terrible business. Bredin's relatives wouldn't hear of Claire or her children
attending it. As the hearse moved off, the horses reared up
and whinnied as if frightened by something, and the coffin
rocked between its shining rails in its glass carriage. The
family spat on the closed door of Claire and Jimmy's house.
A front window was broken. Bredin's mother stood outside
the door and cursed all within it, long and bitter, for having
ruined her son's life. That they might never have luck in this
life, nor peace in the next. That they be blackened with
misery, seed, breed and generation from this day forward.
That they might never have a house where they could live
that was not cursed. That they might see his face every day
and night until the end of their days; her voice weak and
shrill, chanting its sentences in the air to the closed door,
the curtained windows, the hole in the glass of one of them,
until she was finally pulled away.

All was quiet for a time. But then the neighbours said
they began to hear strange noises coming from the house,
like thunder rolling and rattling. The children cried. They
said they couldn't open the front door to go out at times,
because it felt like someone was holding it shut. Claire aged,
and always looked frightened. She went to the priest, but he
said he could do nothing for her until she left Jimmy. Then
Jimmy himself went into the house one day from work. He
had been telling people they were trying to sell it, although

everyone knew it couldn't be sold. Who would want it? Jimmy reappeared that day at the front door, as he had often done, smoking a cigarette and staring at the blank window of the house opposite where Bredin had lived. It was said that, as he flicked the cigarette into the gutter and turned to go in, he hesitated and shouted something – a curse, Bredin's name, something like that – at the blank window. Then he went in. Next morning he was found at the foot of the stairs, his neck broken. The police said it was an accident. Six months later, Claire died in her bed, a look of terror on her face, but not a mark on her body. The children were taken away by Grenaghan's family; the Falkeners wanted nothing to do with them.

But the curse continued. Every house belonging to a Grenaghan or Falkener was haunted. Some days, you couldn't go up the stairs to the bedrooms, or you couldn't get down the stairs from them. No one saw anything – there was just this force that blocked and stopped all movement, that made the house shudder, and left behind it a confused noise as of voices far off, wailing.

People said no one from those families should ever get married. They should be allowed to die out. That was the only way to appease the ghost. Even if they didn't marry, those that remained would always have the presence in their houses. They should emigrate. The boys should become monks, the girls nuns. Anything to stop the revenge. Anything.

So, said Liam, you're as well out of it. That one, Mackey, needs her head examined, staying with Grenaghan. If she stays. And no one who has any sense will get involved with him, as friend or enemy. He's not really a tough – just a fright. Stay away. He has bad blood in him.

'If you believe all that shite,' he added.

RETREAT

March 1954

'. . . denying the whole nature and function of the Retreat.'
These were the President's words. He sat behind his desk,
flanked on one side by the Dean and on the other by Father
Nugent, the Spiritual Director. Moran and I stood before
them, our hands behind our backs, surveying and being
surveyed by the three priests, everybody somewhat perplexed
about what was to come. The President had a clear, kind
face; he believed in being forthright about everything, but
was always at a loss when forthrightness was not quite
what was needed. Father Nugent was distressed, but also
mildly amused. I could see he was not too sorely exercised.
Father McAuley was a different matter. He wanted a punishment. He was small, dark and uncertain of himself. When
he occasionally took us for Latin or Greek, when the usual
teacher was ill or away for some reason, he sometimes made
grammatical mistakes which we were careful to point out to
him in the politest, most diffident ways. Moran and I had
been prominent in these episodes. Now he believed he
had us.

Moran and I had been seen leaving the school grounds
during the Annual Spiritual Retreat and heading off for the
Brandywell football ground to watch the Saturday cup tie
with Linfield, a militantly Protestant team from Belfast. We
were both sorry we had been seen, but not sorry we had
done it, especially as our team had won in the last minute.

The Dean declared that in his opinion physical punishment was not enough. It was over too quickly. Instead, we
were to undergo something more enduring, more in key
with the offence. It had been agreed, he told us, that we
were to undertake a month-long course in Spiritual Reading.

Moran was to be directed by Father Nugent; the Dean was to direct me. The text was to be selections from the *Spiritual Exercises* of St Ignatius Loyola, the founder of the Jesuit order. We were both to stay in after class every day for the month to do this.

Week two, the fourth day, Meditation on Two Standards, the one of Christ, our Commander-in-Chief and Lord; the other of Lucifer, mortal enemy of our human nature. The Dean's method was simple. He chose passages, I learned them by heart, recited them to him, he told me to contemplate them and I went off to commit more to memory. The balanced rationality and fervour of the chosen passages was so exact that I found in them more consolation than the Dean could have wished, even though their clarity was also appalling.

> *The first Point is to imagine as if the chief of all the enemy seated himself in that great field of Babylon, as in a great chair of fire and smoke, in shape horrible and terrifying.*

And against that,

> *The first Point is to consider how Christ our Lord puts himself in a great field of that region of Jerusalem, in lowly place, beautiful and attractive.*

So Satan sends out his demons, Christ his apostles; Satan tempts us with riches, honour, pride; Christ redeems us with poverty, contumely against riches, humility. The rules for making a good and sound election in this life; six points in the First Way and, in the Second Way, four rules and a note. The First Rule is to make the choice out of love of God. In the Second Rule, the exercise was

> *to set before me a man whom I have never seen nor known, and I, desiring all his perfection, to consider what I would tell him to do and elect for the greater*

glory of God our Lord, and the greater perfection of his
soul, and I, doing likewise, to keep the rule which I set
for the other.

The Third and Fourth Rules asked that we consider
what choice we would make were we at the point of death,
or, facing Christ at the Last Judgement, what choice we
would then want to have made.

I recited the passages to him, day in, day out, for a
month, sitting in a straight chair in his room as he sat in an
armchair, scanning the text as I spoke. He wearied of it long
before I did. Loyola was equipped for difficulty and terror;
the Dean was not. He nodded every so often at my recital
but was concerned only I get the words perfect, not with
what they might mean.

The *Exercises* were clean and tonic. A man grew out of
them, one whom I had never seen nor known, in all perfection, making choices in accord with that perfection. He was
a star, sure and yet troubled, but always reducing his trouble
gradually by accumulating certainty, by making decision after
decision, knowing the more, the more trouble it took him
to know. But when I imagined him so, then I would see
myself again in a dither of light and dark, see my father
again, see Eddie, re-recognise my mother, see them blur and
fade, know that I too was blurred, was astray for not knowing
how to choose. I lay awake at night, with the book open
beside my pillow, my brothers sleeping in the dark, the roar
of the football crowd humming in my ears as the final goal
went in, the Dean reappearing in the classroom, and a nervous radar starting a scan inside me, sensing the incoming
fire, the choices hurtling faster out of Loyola's Babylon,
Jerusalem, homing in.

BROTHEL

April 1954

Right beside the boys' entrance to the football ground, there was a house that always had the window blinds drawn and was reputed to be a brothel. Liam claimed that it certainly was, that he knew for a fact the names of the men who went there and the names of some of the women too. One man, in particular, a Post Office Inspector called Charlie McCabe, went there every Tuesday. McCabe was a prominent figure in diocesan work – collecting money for charities and forever, as Liam said, buttering up the ecclesiastics. A slime-bag. I didn't believe him. He and I, Toner and Harkin had an argument about it. It finished with my agreeing, for a bet, to go to the house and 'flush McCabe out'.

I was to get two shillings if I went up to the door, knocked and asked for 'my uncle', Charlie McCabe, pretending he was wanted in an emergency. If I didn't get McCabe to come to the door, Liam kept the money. He held the money out in his open palm to show me it was a real bet, and said, 'Off you go.' I went down the cul-de-sac to the last house on the left. The blinds were drawn on the two front windows that were separated by the door. I knocked. There was a long pause, and the door was opened by a young woman with tousled hair, wearing a blue blouse and skirt. Her mouth was scarlet with lipstick. When she asked me what I wanted I said I was calling for my uncle, Charlie McCabe, for he was needed in an emergency. His daughter had had an accident, I said. She looked at me half-smilingly and asked what sort of accident. Stupidly, I was not prepared for that one. His daughter's sick, I said quickly. She might have to go to hospital. She left me at the door and vanished down the short hall and into the living room. I heard her talking and then laughing. A man's head came round the door, looked at me and withdrew. More voices. Then another man appeared, short and burly, buckling – or was it unbuckling? – his belt. He wore a collarless, striped shirt and moleskin trousers. He stood about a foot away from me and asked who I was. I gave him a false name – Rory Harkin. Where was I from? Again, I lied. Rossville Street. There were no Harkins in Rossville Street, he said very casually, both hands still on the loose ends of his belt. I took a step back. And Charlie McCabe wasn't in the house, he said. He was never in that house. And he had no daughter. At that, he and I moved together. His grasping hand ran down the front of my shirt as I jumped back, the belt came whistling off him and I ran towards the street corner where the others were already turning to run. We didn't stop until we were back within our own territory of the sloping streets. As we passed the top of Beechwood Street, we passed Larry, standing there, his hands in his pockets, staring up Bligh's Lane as usual. Liam said a visit to the brothel would do Larry a world of good. All that stuff about the she-devil gave him a pain. The man was just scared of sex, like most of the older people. I stared at Larry. He was utterly immobile. I could understand someone being afraid of sex. It made me think of fire, glinting with greed and danger.

'It was worth two bob, anyway,' said Liam, hefting the coins in his hand. 'We split it, a bob each. I organised it, you did it.'

Was that house really a brothel? That's what the whisper was. Was that McCabe? Liam wanted to know. He hadn't stayed long enough to see; all he saw was the man coming out with the belt in one hand and his other hand out to grab me. No, it wasn't McCabe, I answered. Someone else. All I could remember was his hands on the buckle of his belt. Nor did I know the young woman, but I remembered her, all of her: her sleepy air, her half-smile, her red, red, mouth. What would it be like with her? I couldn't imagine. No. I could. But that was what I should not do. Look what had happened to Larry McLaughlin, standing at the foot of Bligh's Lane and never speaking. For protection, I whispered St Ignatius to myself in the back bedroom:

> *In the persons who go from mortal sin to mortal sin, the enemy is commonly used to propose to them apparent pleasures, making them imagine sensual delights and pleasures in order to hold them more and make them grow in their vices and sins.*

And still the vision of that young woman drifted there, vague one moment, the next vivid, reaching for me, unloosing the clasp of her skirt that rustled down as I leapt back and came forward, blurring inwardly, making my election.

KATIE

May 1954

Katie had been in England, her first time away, because her daughter Maeve had married there. There had been great whispering and secrecy about it – why she wasn't coming home to get married, as would have been usual; why only Katie went over, although all the rest of her brothers and sisters had been invited. 'She married a black man,' Liam told me, 'and they say he's not even a Christian, never mind a Catholic. So, everybody to the barricades and hide behind them. Katie's great, though. She hates it, but she wouldn't not go, even though she's terrified of travelling on her own.' The marriage was in Luton, a place we only knew of because it had a football team – of sorts.

When she returned, Katie talked non-stop for a week about England, Luton, trains, ships, the wedding breakfast, Maeve and her husband, Marcus, the apartment they lived in, how happy they were – on and on. But her chatter was of no use. My mother disapproved, told Katie that she wished Maeve well, but it was not a Christian marriage, no good would come of it. They argued furiously. Finally, Katie declared she was never coming back to our house and left, slamming the door behind her.

She stayed away for ages. But then the news came that Maeve was pregnant. Katie was thrown by the prospect of a grandchild. She fussed and worried, talked about nothing else. My mother caused another breach when she said she was worried that Marcus might now leave Maeve. History would repeat itself. As McIlhenny had ditched Katie, so Marcus would ditch Maeve. As I walked Katie home from our house late one night, she fumed about the notion. There was no comparison, she told me. For in her case, something

172

strange had happened. She wasn't quite the fool my mother took her for. She wondered what that something was. Had I ever heard anything? Had my grandfather ever mentioned McIlhenny to me in those days before he died? I told her no. Her father, she said, had been really nice to her after McIlhenny left, but for one thing. He wouldn't hear of her going out to Chicago after him; said he was a no-good; said they couldn't afford it; said she couldn't travel when pregnant. That might have been true enough. But Katie had the impression more than money was the problem; he never once said McIlhenny would come back, as if he knew there was no chance of that. But how did he know?

I shook my head. I resolved to say nothing, to stay dumb. Katie snuffled into her handkerchief as we reached her door. It's all coming out now, she announced, as she went out to the scullery to put on the kettle. She had never been forgiven, not by her father, not by her own sister – my mother – and, sorry though she was to have to tell me . . . but then who else could she talk to except her daughter, Maeve, and Maeve was away, and it was through her that she, Katie, was being punished again for something that was no fault of her own. For her sister to talk like that, about Maeve being left by her husband, as if it were some curse in the family, some punishment she had to bear for what her husband had done to her. And where, she asked me angrily, where was that same sister when my daughter was married? Where was my family when I had to travel to England alone for Maeve's wedding? If that's not punishment, I don't know what is. And then still to be flinty when I come back, to be so flinty I can't even tell her my daughter's pregnant without having all those wounds re-opened with all this 'like mother, like daughter', 'you were left behind, she'll be left behind'.

She paused for a moment. I made to go, but she went on even as she stood up to go to the door with me.

It's years of spite, that's what it is, she said. Just because McIlhenny dropped her when she was twenty-six and married me when I was eighteen – that's what it's about. That's why she's so taken up with the idea of Maeve getting ditched the way I was. Because she was ditched herself. And me sympathising with her and promising never to tell your father about McIlhenny. That's what I get. I wiped her eye with that man, though God knows I wish I hadn't, and I kept my promise; I said nothing about him until this day, and there she is taking it out on me through Maeve, *his* daughter and *my* daughter. Don't for Christ's sake talk to me about religion. I'll lay a bet that black man Marcus'll be a lot better to Maeve than any of the religious gets she might have met here – or than the very religious white man I married, living out there in Chicago and going to Mass every Sunday of the year.

'There now,' she said, as she held the door open, 'there's the last story I'll tell you or any of you children. I'm glad it was a true one for a change.'

PART THREE

PART THREE

CHAPTER FIVE

RELIGIOUS KNOWLEDGE

September 1954

'How long,' asked the teacher of religious knowledge, 'does it take a flea to crawl through a barrel of tar?'

'Six weeks?' I hazarded.

'Wrong,' he answered, striking me, not very hard, across the face with the back of his hand. 'Try again.'

'Six months?'

'You don't get the point, do you?' He pulled on my hair, not hard, bringing my head towards the wood of the desk, then letting me go. He walked up the aisle to the blackboard.

'I'll write the answer on the board, so that you may all the better understand it.' With what seemed like real weariness, he scrawled on the board the words 'Amiens Street Station'.

He faced us. We gazed at him. He pointed at me.

'Confound me. Disagree with the answer.'

'I can't disagree with what I don't understand, Father.'

'Implying you can't agree with it either?'

'I can do neither.'

'Good. This is a condition to be sought for. It is the condition of being educated. Let's try again. How many angels can balance on the head of a pin? This, I warn you, is a traditional query and not at all eccentric.'

'Balance, Father, is not a requirement of angels.'

'No? You have seraphic access that I lack.'

I remained quiet. I did not know what his last remark meant.

'Once more. In steps this time. Do you agree that, when we speak of a ghost, we imply the preceding existence of something or someone corporeal? That is, something or someone having had a body before that thing or person achieved ghostliness? Yes or no?'

'Yes, Father.'

'Tell me, then, who or what was the Holy Ghost before he was a ghost?'

I was silent. To the left of me, Alec McShane laughed. The teacher frowned.

'We are dealing here with a theological conundrum, of signal importance. Hardly the occasion for another display of the idiocy of rural life. I would like an answer.'

He pointed at me again.

'I can't say, Father. I don't have an answer.'

'Good. On the first question, you don't understand the answer. On the second, you deny the validity of the question. On the third, you have no answer. I hope now you can see why religion is different. My chief desire is to let you see that there is that which is rational, that which is irrational and that which is non-rational – and to leave you weltering in that morass thereafter. I shall thereby do the State some service and the Church even more. Doctrine, dogma and decision – these you can live by so that you may avoid the disintegration of the mind. Not a serious threat, I have to say, for many *in* this or *of* this class of person ranked so monotonously before me.'

This man's father was a Papal Knight. He was Sir Roy Creedon. *Sir.* I was enraged, but my rage made me smile. He was right, this was education.

His Roman collar glistened white around his plump throat. He was much given to sighing, expanding his soutane above his cummerbund. Sir Roy drove a Rover car. Roy of the Rover. Only Sir Roy and the police had cars. Knights in shining armour. Papal and anti-Papal Knights.

'If your geography teacher told you faith could move mountains, you might evince some surprise. If your mathematics teacher told you that in any given series, the first would be last, and the last would be first, you might think him inebriated. But I can tell you these things in sobriety and you shall believe them. All I ask is that you learn to do so without attempting to understand them. Once we had here, in Ireland, the simple faith of the peasant. Now, thanks to free education and godless socialism, we shall have the simple faith of the proletariat. There is no need to exhort you people to be simple. You achieve that condition effortlessly. But I shall, in this and in succeeding years, exhort you to believe that education can be conducted in such manner as to confirm that simplicity rather than disturb it. It is, of course, a gratuitous exercise, but one demanded by the society of which you form such a happily disenfranchised part. Now I wish to be silent and so must you be until the class bell relieves us of the burden of one another's presence.'

And we sat silent while he stood with his back to us, gazing out of the window, perfectly still.

ALL OF IT?

November 1954

A choice, an election, was to be made between what actually happened and what I imagined, what I had heard, what I kept hearing. There was a story about one of the IRA men in the distillery strapping himself to an upright iron girder at the corner of the building as it caught fire. He had a machine-gun, probably a Thompson, and he blazed away with that as the police came shadowing across the street below to the base of the building. He was about twenty feet up and the bullets sprayed from the Thompson as from a hose with a filter nozzle, all over the place. But the gunman was such a target, silhouetted by the fire, stock-still in one place. He must have been hit twenty or thirty times, and his figure stood there, drooped on the girder, glittering when the flames shone on the blood that soaked his front, his arms straight down before him. I didn't remember his name. His body disappeared when the whiskey vats exploded, and the whole building began to buckle and fall in on itself.

Still, that was just a detail. Maybe I had imagined and should try to forget it. While that was going on, if it was going on, what else was happening? Some of the men inside the building had got out before the cordon was completed, running — maybe even walking casually — through the network of backstreets, heading for a safe house. Eddie had kept his gun throughout that escape — a First-World-War rifle that had belonged to a Black-and-Tan soldier killed in the War of Independence, three years before, in County Tipperary. Was it Dan who had said this? Or Katie? Or Grandfather? I didn't know. I could hear all their voices in the kitchen but I couldn't match a voice to a detail. This made it hard to think it through. Much of it must have been ornament, people making strange little alliances in their heads between things they had heard or read about, seeking to assert themselves in those endless conversations, implying they were in the know, there was much else they could tell but . . .

The year was 1922. Late spring. That was for sure. Eddie's parents, my father's parents, had died in December 1921. Billy Mahon had gone over the bridge in November 1921. My father's sisters had been eight months in that farmhouse; they had been sent there about February 1922, got out of there in November. That's when they told my father about Eddie and the hooded men who came with him that night. So he had known all that length of time what he thought was the whole story. And my mother had known McIlhenny about that time; had been out with him. Then he had dropped her for Katie, whom he married in 1926. She got pregnant soon afterwards. And Sergeant Burke, or someone in the police, had got him out to Chicago in July that same year, after a tip-off – to my grandfather? By whom? My mother met my father some years later – about 1930. They didn't get married for a long time – they had no money, no prospects. He's still boxing. They married in 1935. What did she know when they met, when they married? Did she know about Eddie then? Did she know about McIlhenny? I was fairly sure not; she couldn't have known anything, otherwise she wouldn't have been so shocked that day she came down from Grandfather's bedroom, saying Eddie's name and crying. But I didn't know what she knew when she married my father. I wondered if I wanted to know. Still, I'd reserve that and work out the rest first.

So they got to the safe house – how many of them? Grandfather, Larry, Eddie and maybe the traitor himself, McIlhenny. Perhaps others. There was a meeting of some kind, an inquiry. There was a stool-pigeon somewhere, yes, someone had passed information. They moved from the house and went out to Donegal, through the new border country. They had to get over the border quickly. Had they a car? Did they go in some kind of cart? Were there horses? But I knew where they went. To the feud-farm, the one family home Eddie had left. That's where he was interrogated. That was at the heart of the feud. For when his aunt and uncle were told to take Eddie's young sisters and themselves out to the shed beside the hen-house and to stay there until they were told to come out, and when they heard, for they must have heard, the shouting and screaming, they turned cold on Eddie and Eddie's family. Perhaps they had seen him being taken away. Ena and Bernadette were whimpering and terrified. The aunt and uncle were terrified. They were told to say nothing. If they reported anything, they'd be seen to, as their traitorous nephew was going to be seen to. Bernadette and Ena had heard that, or something to that effect. They knew they weren't going to see Eddie again. Anyway, the aunt and uncle had repeated it to them, called them republican gets, informers' spawn, all sorts of things. It was some time after that, I guess, they banished the two young sisters to the shed and treated them as skivvies. And it was this that my father had discovered months later. His sisters were almost stupefied by then, by shock, fright, tyranny. Eight months of it. It was Bernadette who brought her sister Ena to Derry one night, asking him for refuge, and told him the truth about their existence there and the truth about Eddie. And the row I remembered from childhood in that same farmhouse – that was twenty-three years later when the aunt had died, and a solicitor had informed my father that she had left some possessions of his parents to him in her will, possessions she had taken from their house the week they died and had kept since. But he never got them. The uncle – he was only an uncle by marriage – refused to hand anything over and declared my father could see him in court where he would publicly expose Eddie, whose name was still good in most people's minds. Not that my father would have had the money to go to law anyway. Nor could he have faced the public exposure of his brother. So he had swept us up and out. And then, years later, brought

Liam and me close to it and told us about the Field of the Disappeared. And I had jeered at him.

And in the farmhouse that night? Eddie must have known he was in trouble. He had known more than anyone else who was directly involved. He had somehow got away. Who else could have told the police? My grandfather? One of the senior men? Impossible. Had Eddie told anyone else? No. They must all have had their alibis, their confidence, their suspicions. Did they beat him? Tie him up? Burn him with cigarettes? Keep hitting him on the head with a limp, heavy book? That was a way of banging someone around but keeping him conscious. Was that one of the books I had seen on those shelves? Even so, Eddie couldn't have confessed, not when he was innocent and not when he knew that someone else, maybe one of his interrogators, was the real informer. So they took him out of the farmhouse and they moved across the countryside to Grianan, reaching it when dark had fallen. They put him in the secret passage inside the walls, rolled the stone across the entrance and sat there on the grass floor, smoking and discussing what they would do. Then, maybe, Grandfather took out a revolver and handed it to Larry and told him to go in and do it. And Larry crawled down the passageway to the space where Eddie sat on the wishing-chair, and he hunkered before Eddie and he looked at him and, maybe, said something, maybe, told him to say his prayers and then he shot him, several times or maybe just once, and the fort boomed as though it were hollow. How did the others hear it, sitting or standing out there on the grassy floor of the fort? Maybe it was just a crack, or several cracks, in the air. Maybe they heard Eddie's voice before the shot. Did they leave his body there overnight? Did Larry make him kneel and shoot him in the brainstem from behind? Did Larry tell him it was all right, he could go now, and let him go on ahead and then shoot Eddie as he bent down to crawl out the passage? No one would ever know because that was the night Larry met the devil-woman and stopped speaking. He had just handed the gun to Grandfather without a word and gone off down the dark path to make his way home while the others went back to Donegal.

It was hard to believe that Larry had never talked. When he left his post at the Lone Moor corner and went home for his tea, he must have talked then, inside his own house, to his ancient mother, to his unmarried brother, Willie, who worked in the slaughterhouse. But no, the word was that he never talked. His brother wasn't much better. He'd talk about the weather or the price of meat or greyhound racing, but beyond that, nothing. You could stand in front of Larry and talk into his face for ten minutes and all you'd get would be a shifting of his eyes from your face down to his shoes and back up again. The man who had had sex with the devil. The man who had killed my father's brother. All on the same night. There he stood, dark in his shiny suit, his neat shirt, buttoned at the neck, the same greasy tie twisted like a tongue inside his V-necked pullover, his small feet in black shoes with polished toecaps, his hands in his pockets, his sharp face grey and odourless under his peaked cap. You could look at Larry a thousand times, envisage him a thousand times, and still you had to look at him again the next time you passed to assure yourself that he was there, alive and inanimate, buried upright in the dead air that encased him.

What did the others do with the body? Bury it near there, carry it all the way back and dump it into the river, over the bridge? That seemed unlikely. Grandfather hadn't told me, and I had forgotten to ask. Was there anyone left alive who knew where the body was? And all the time McIlhenny maybe was at home; maybe he was out for a walk with my mother or sitting in her house, yarning away with her, putting everyone on notice that he had come to call for her. And all that time Burke was in his barracks, knowing what might happen, hoping it would, remembering Billy Mahon. And the distillery smouldered into the dawn, surprising the seagulls who came in from the docks to soar around it and cry away from its heat and smell.

My mother's father had my father's brother killed. She had known that now, since just before Grandfather died. My father didn't know it at all. My mother had gone out with McIlhenny, the traitor who had set Eddie up for execution. My father did not know that. And McIlhenny had dropped her and married Katie, her sister. Then he had been tipped off and fled to Chicago. Katie didn't know that. Nor did my father. My mother had always known that McIlhenny had fled, had known he was an informer. Her father must have told her that; what he hadn't told her, not until just before he died, was the truth about what had happened to Eddie. She knew it all now. She knew I knew it too. And she wasn't going to tell any of it. Nor was I. But she didn't like me for knowing it. And my father thought he had told me everything. I could tell him nothing, though I hated him not knowing. But only my mother could tell him. No one else. Was it her way of loving him, not telling him? It was my way of loving them both, not telling either. But knowing what I did separated me from them both.

CRAZY JOE

January 1955

It was Crazy Joe who almost completed the story for me. He was regularly consigned for periods to Gransha, the local asylum. Yet when he came out again, he always seemed more disturbed, more upset.

'God's only excuse is that he does not exist,' Joe announced to me, banging his stick on the railings outside the Public Library. 'Isn't that a good one, young Caliban, eh?'

He had a long egg-stain plunged down his shirt. His eyes foamed. The woman in charge of the library had had him removed by two of the park-keepers because of the noise he was making and because he had once more started to pull books from the shelves and throw them on the floor, shouting that they were rubbish, tosh, garbage. I had followed him outside and watched him stomping up and down on the cinder path in a fury, whacking the rhododendron bushes with his stick in a manic rage, roaring curses into the air. When he finally noticed me, he beamed and came rushing forward, dragging at my shirt-sleeve, cupping his hand round the back of my neck, dragging me down towards his disoriented face.

'Who do you think wrote that, now? Not in one of your stupid poets, I can tell you that. Will you ever grow up? You're taller than you were and still you're so, *so* stupid. No sign of improvement anywhere. You fancy the women, I bet? Sweet Christ! By the sufferings of the Desert Fathers, by the anguish of Judas, will you ever learn anything, shall ye be redeemed in this our bollocks of an existence, you futile creature?'

His small shoulders heaved up and down, and his face

ballooned with anger. He stared at me but his eyes were so flickery and disturbed I guessed he could see little clearly.

'As for that bitch who had me thrown out again, by Jesus I'll see her in hell, I'll burn the whole damned library down one of these days, on the illiterate, ignorant, sexless whore! Pagan! Pagan fanatic!'

Then, composing himself, he lifted a finger and intoned, 'The valuable library of Alexandria was pillaged or destroyed; and, near twenty years afterwards, the appearance of the empty shelves excited the regret and indignation of every spectator whose mind was not totally darkened by religious prejudice.'

Then he shook his head and stopped. 'That's a good one, religious prejudice. He should have lived here, then he'd have seen . . . '

With another shake of the head, he turned away.

'Waste of time!' he snarled.

Then he faced me again, his breath winding down, leaning on his stick, pushing his false teeth in and out, his face calming and paling.

'Do you know what?' He smiled. 'I'd like nothing better than a walk around the lily pond, if you'd let me lean on your arm. Then we'll be right as rain.'

We went round, slowly, his breathing still rancorous in his chest, but easing.

'The mere proximity of the past ruins my indigestion, young fella. I hope you can understand that. I think you do; it ruins your own, I know to look at you. Spiritual constipation. I want to teach you something. But do me one favour. Repay me by not always being such a young idiot. Don't spend your life as a pupil. It's insulting. You're always running around like a dog, sniffing at the arse of every secret, a dirty habit. Copulate if you must. Get it over and done with. Then grow up. Now, let my arm go. I want a rest.'

He gazed at the water lilies as he leaned on the railing.

'Lilies that fester. O Shenandoah! Your wee sister, dead. I loved your daughter, Mister. Orange lilies. Lilliesbullero! . . . You never say anything to me worth hearing but you hear lots from me that's worth saying. All a waste. And now, after this, when they report I was thrown out of the library again, what'll they do, my lovely family? They'll put me away again, with all the wrecks, and they'll beat the living daylights out of me in there, those male nurses. May they slow-burn in hell!'

I knew he had spent long periods in the local asylum, which had a cruel reputation. The only difference between the nurses and the inmates, they said, was the uniform. He was right. I had nothing to say to him. He always left me stranded, my head excited, my heart slow.

'And what,' he asked me, turning his large head sideways on his small body, winching it round like a clockwork toy, 'and what now do you know that you didn't know when I first took you into the art room in there? You needn't answer. I know. Who was it first told you about Larry? Who was it pointed you in the right direction? No need to answer. You know. Where did it happen? Boom-boom. Its vast out-rollings, forever and ever amen. Up the aery mountain, rushing down again, they said he saw the devil, pathetic little men. Eh?'

He was talking about Larry. I knew that instantly. If I say nothing, I thought, he might go on. But then, equally, he might fling up his arms, drop his stick, tell me to retrieve it for him, take it and stomp off. He was beginning to get excited again. One of the park attendants who had helped remove Joe from the library was passing at the other side of the pond, glancing sidelong at us. He was ready to intervene if Joe should try to go back in. Joe saw him too.

'Henry Patterson,' he said, 'that's who that is. Forty years of age and he has reached the peak of his career, throwing an old man like me out of a library. A strong bastard. He has hands like tree roots. When he caught me by the shoulder in there, he near took the bones out in his claw. May arthritis blight him and leave him with hands like door-knobs.'

We watched Patterson stroll on, continuing his wide circuit around us. We began to walk again, Joe balancing one hand on my arm. He wanted to sit by the rose-beds, so we headed for the park bench nearby. He sat there, mopping his face with a large white handkerchief, although it was a cloudy and not especially warm day.

'I'd cry if I could,' he said. 'The hanky helps sometimes to bring it on. But not today, not today. Console me with a story or even a song. Yes, that'd be better. You know no stories worth hearing. Sing instead. A nice, low song. Don't scare the birds, mind.'

We leaned in together, and I sang him 'Sweet Afton'. At the second verse, he began to cry but shook my arm, nodding at me to go on.

> *My Mary's asleep*
> *By yon murmuring stream,*
> *Flow gently Sweet Afton,*
> *Disturb not her dream.*

'Ah, dear,' he sighed when I had done, 'murder it as you may, young Caliban, it's still a sweet song. Do you know "The Quiet Land of Erin"?'

I sang him that too, watching as I did for the approach of anyone, for that would have silenced me at once. But no one came near. Then he sang a couple of the lines to himself, his hands on the knees of his black priest-like trousers.

> *And 'tis I would let the Sunday go*
> *In the cuckoo-glen above the bay.*

I watched a rose petal fall and skid on the grass for a bit before it rested, uneasily.

'Sundays,' said Joe, 'are terrible days. Everything terrible that I know happened on a Sunday. Isn't that strange? You'd know that yourself, with your family history. Fire on a Saturday, execution on a Sunday. Or was the fire on a Friday?

191

You'd not think I'd forget something like that now. Well I remember that day. Never heard so many shots in my life. But the Sunday, that I'm sure of. No, it started on a Sunday, that's it.'

'What started on a Sunday?'

He chanted, in a light, parodic voice:

> Twas on a Sunday we asked him why,
> Twas on a Monday he had to die . . .

I was silent for a moment.

'Were you there, then? On the Sunday? Or the day of the shoot-out?'

He mused for a while, resting his hands on the stick, lowering his chin on his hands. He opened his mouth wide once or twice.

'Sure who wasn't there, wherever there was, that time. Everybody who mattered was there, all linked in, dancing to somebody else's tune, if only they knew it. I was a young man, then. Not so mad then, I think, but on my way, on my way.'

He paused for a moment.

'So young Maeve's got married, I hear? And to a blackie as well! I'd have liked to see her father's face when he heard that!'

He cackled in his indifferent way.

'You could hardly see his face, since he's in Chicago this long time,' I replied.

'Oh, I still see his face, never you fear. Four in the morning. The eighth of July 1926. Getting out of the police car, like a shadow. Two men in the back. And our dear old friend Burke at the wheel. McIlhenny stops to pull up his collar and I step out, so I do, from the wall where I'd been standing out of the rain and I look close and I see who it is and off I go, like a shadow up the street and leave him standing there in the rain.'

'So what was he doing there?'

'What the hell do you think he was doing? Informing. Informing. Selling his people for a few shillings. I'll tell you this. He never saw me. But he got out in time. Never saw his wife or child again after that. But who tipped him off that he had been seen? Can't work that one out for sure, though I have my notions. I'm surprised the police bothered to take care of him. He was of use to them once in his life and never again.' Then he spread his arms and sang

Goodnight sweetheart, we'll be waiting for you,
Goodnight sweetheart, you will soon be sorry . . .

He got up. I handed him his stick.

'I'm off,' he announced, 'and when I see you again, you'll be a lot older. But I'll be the same age as ever I was.'

He tapped his forehead with his finger, beaming at me.

'Eternal youth. The secret of the insane.'

He took a step away, turned round again.

'That's what punishment does; makes you remember everything.'

He moved off along the path, humming to himself, and I stayed for a moment to watch the rose petal lodged precariously in the grass, straining to catch the next whiff of the breeze. So that was the tip-off, Joe? Joe identified McIlhenny as the informer? It seemed unlikely, but there it was.

IN IRISH

October 1955

My mother knew no Irish, but she had dismembered bits
and pieces of poems and songs that were from the Irish.
When she had been ill, she had asked me once if I knew
any of the old poems in Irish, if I had learned them at
school. But I knew very little. There was one, she said, that
was by a woman, and in it the woman lamented that she
had done a terrible thing, she had forsaken the man she loved,
but she could still remember how, before this had happened,
the trees in the wood made wild music to her, and the sound
of the sea was such that it hurt her breast with its rolling.
Did I know that poem? The woman's name was Líadan. She
thought there might be a song about it. But I didn't know.
Why did she forsake him? I asked. She didn't know, except
that it had to do with gaining entry to Paradise.

I decided to tell her everything I knew. But every time
I started, my courage failed. I thought if I could just get
going, I'd get through it all. Anything might happen. Maybe
she would put her hands over her ears and start crying. Or
worse. But I had to say I knew. The truth was swollen inside
me. I thought of telling Liam but that seemed wrong, unless
I had told her first. Then I could tell him, if she allowed it.
Several times I tried, but I couldn't.

I decided to write it all out in an exercise book, partly
to get it clear, partly to rehearse it and decide which details to
include or leave out. But then the fear that someone would
find it and read it overcame me. So, with the help of a
dictionary, I translated it all into Irish, taking more than
a week to do it. Then I destroyed the English version,
burning it in front of my mother's eyes, even though she
told me I would clog up the fire with the paper.

I waited for a few days. Then, one evening, when my father was there, reading his way through *Pear's Encyclopaedia*, his hand-held education, as he called it, and I was sitting at the table doing homework, I read it all outright in Irish to him. It was an essay we had been assigned in school, I told him, on local history. He just nodded and smiled and said it sounded wonderful. My mother had listened carefully. I knew she knew what I was doing. My father tapped me on the shoulder and said he liked to hear the language spoken in the house. When he went out to sweep the backyard, I could feel her looking at me, though my back was turned to her. She was quiet for a long time. I watched him through the window, sloshing water from a bucket on the concrete and then sweeping vigorously. She got up with a sigh and made to move towards the stairs. He had stopped brushing and was leaning on the handle, staring at the ground. She was looking at him too, I knew. Then she said something very brief, maybe something angry, that I couldn't hear because I was crying.

We heard that Sergeant Burke's two sons, his only children, had gone off to Maynooth to study for the priesthood. At least no more Burkes would be bred, said Uncle Tom. I wouldn't bet on that, said his brother Dan. They just won't carry the name, that's all. My mother stirred from her torpor to ask God to forgive Dan for saying such a thing about the holy priests. Everybody laughed. Such a family for the black uniform, said someone else. Don't, said my mother, don't dare associate one with the other. They belong in different worlds, different worlds.

POLITICAL EDUCATION

November 1956

We stared at the speaker, a priest in British army uniform, a chaplain, a smooth and tall man, with a tall and smooth accent, a handsome face tinged a little with blood-pressure at the cheeks, a visitor to our school, introduced by the President, sent by the Ministry of Education. He seemed to me exquisite as he put on his peaked cap, shook hands with the teachers on the platform, folded his papers, smiled at the hesitant applause. He bowed slightly at us, brought his hands together in a prayerful gesture, and, after thanks and acknow-ledgements to the President and to the college, began his speech.

'Were you to view the Foyle Basin from Binevenagh, almost twelve hundred feet above the sea, with the bird-haunted mud flats of the River Roe at its foot, you would begin to appreciate both the beauty and the strategic impor-tance of the dramatic landscape and seascape in which your city rests. This was the city that, even today, still commands the eastern approaches of the North Atlantic, that is still a vital port for the great NATO fleets that regularly put in here during those exercises that are part of the Western world's preparations for the defeat of the international Com-munist threat. That threat is as real now as once was the threat of those German submarines that surrendered here at the end of the war and now lie rusting on the ocean floor, their scuttling a symbol and reminder of our determination to defend the cause of democracy and freedom, of the might and resolve with which we shall always mobilise our resources to maintain that democratic system in which we all have the good fortune to live. As the Soviet submarines glide under the waters of the North Atlantic today, as the sailors of many lands arrive in Derry to add to the rich fabric of the city's life, you will remember the signs of the war the city has seen – the scores of German prisoners, the gallant survivors of U-boat attacks, the lines of captured German submarines, the hundreds of American and British warships, the great American naval base of 1941 that still remains, those German warplanes in their bombing of the city that mercifully was to survive and remain thereafter beyond their reach – all of these dramatic sights that attest to the proud role your city played in that titanic struggle. And once more you are called to take part in a battle that is just as dramatic, although less visible: a struggle against a foe that is no less real for being less visible. This is a battle for the hearts and minds of men; a battle of faithlessness against faith; a battle of subtle wiles against manly freedom; a battle of cold atheism against the genial warmth of that Christian faith that has lit so many Irish hearts down the centuries. Not for them, not for such a people, the closed churches, the prison camps, the expropriated lands of a secular and military state, the fruit of a godless creed. Atheism is against not only our reason but our instincts. It cannot long prevail. Ireland has never elected such evil, for Ireland and the Irish people trust, and properly trust, their deepest instincts. With their co-habitants of these islands, they shall put away – as a distraction and a disablement – whatever there is of local dispute, of transient division between them, and look instead, in a higher and nobler view, to those sunlit uplands of human freedom that are the ribbed slopes of Binevenagh and the wide plateau that stretches beyond it from these contested waters to the security of our inland towns and villages. Our internal disputes are no more than family quarrels; faced with an external enemy, the solidarity of our Christian family must reassert itself, be galvanised to protect, as each part of the variegated Irish family has protected down through the centuries, its own essential freedoms. We have many memorials of the Irish urge to defend those freedoms – from the walls of this city itself to the ancient fortress of Grianan that surveys the ancient hinterland of Columba's monastic settlement that brought Christianity to the neighbouring island. With such a history, with such a land, with such a people – famously generous as enemies, famously faithful as allies – we can face into the future with confidence, conscious that the wild rolling seas of the distant Atlantic are as vital a part of our domain as the very streets on which we walk, the monuments that we preserve, the affections that we nourish. I know that what your city has done in the war that is past, it shall do again in the war that has already arrived and has still to be won in the future. It is an onerous responsibility. Yet it is a matter of personal pride and happiness that this responsibility is to be borne by the people of the city I first came to know during the war at the Combined Naval and Air Headquarters at Magee College and that I have visited regularly ever since. It is here, where fashion and fads are treated with amusement and contempt, here, in a society that is rooted in tradition and continuity, that one can have a sense of the links between the human struggle and the eternal verities. Without that abiding sense of continuity, men would become little better than the flies of a summer. With that as a treasured element of our patrimony, we become actors in a great drama, a story that ends in a world beyond our own and for which our own is an immense and glorious preparation. God is the goal of our history; our history is the preserve of the God-fearing, the brave, the chivalric, the courteous, the humble. I salute you all.'

We filed away to our classes from the main hall. Everyone was curiously silent.

Next day, in history class, we discussed the speech. Father McAuley asked for initial reactions, but got none. Had we not listened? he shouted. Did we not pay attention? Were we vegetable, animal or mineral? Did we not see any connection between this man's visit and the recent bombing campaign?

To stop him flying off into one of his furies, Irwin intervened to ask what was all that stuff about Binevenagh?

What had that to do with Communism? Slightly appeased, but still emanating that mildly contemptuous patience that marked all his addresses to us, McAuley explained that by mentioning Binevenagh the man had been able to give us an overall view both of the area and of the situation. He had started with something we knew, then went on to connect that with what we didn't know. That was a pedagogic technique, he told us. We had to write those words down. Again there was silence. Exasperated, McAuley then told us that the lecture had been designed to lift our eyes from our own petty squabbles and let us see our place in the world at large. The man had vision. Well McAuley remembered those same U-boats lined up out at Lisahally; well he remembered the American ships in the lough; well he remembered this, that and the other. We roiled internally in boredom. McShane then asked if the man was a Catholic priest. Certainly not, answered McAuley, the man was an Anglican, or what was called an Anglo-Catholic priest, although as far as he was concerned – and us too – there was no kind of Catholic other than the Roman Catholic. He told us this every year. So we should never use the term 'Anglo-Catholic', for that was admitting that the Reformation had right on its side. This distinction left us awash. So which was worse, I asked, Communism or the Reformation? Both were bad, but the Reformation was history. Communism was the living threat. But are we not threatened by the Reformation here, even yet? Isn't it held against you here to be a Catholic? That was just what the lecturer was telling us, he explained, with no sense of unease. Forget those old distinctions. That was a family quarrel within the Christian family. It would work itself out. When that had all been resolved, Communism would still be there, threatening anyone who believed in God. We were of the West and must throw our lot in with it. Locked into our little streets, he told us, we lacked that promontory view the man had described, but as long as we kept our faith we would, just by doing that, play our role in the world. We must recognise the irrelevance of our own

199

internal differences in face of the demands of world history. That's where we should set our eyes – on the global horizon. And next day, we would continue with our regular European history. The Congress of Vienna. History was about trends, not about people. We had to learn to see the trends. Though God knows it was unlikely, for all his efforts and those of the lecturer, that we ever would. He rushed out as the bell rang to smoke his cigarette in the corridor outside before the next class came in.

'Propaganda,' said Irwin. 'That's all that is. First, it's the Germans. Then it's the Russians. Always, it's the IRA. British propaganda. What have the Germans or Russians to do with us? It's the British who are the problem for us. McAuley's a moron.'

I remembered the teenage German my father had brought extra lunch to when he was in the prisoner-of-war compound down at the docks and who had, I had been told, given my father the German pistol as a thank you – the pistol that had disappeared into the police barracks years before and ignited so much since. But that was a petty squabble, perhaps. I was beginning to catch on at last. Global vision. I needed that.

SERGEANT BURKE

December 1957

Look now, Ma'am, Sergeant Burke had said to my mother (or something like that), I'm not bringing you any more trouble so rest easy. We've got a lot of things on file that I want to clear up and put away for good, and they date back before my time as sergeant here. Oh, she couldn't tell me rightly how he had said it all, it just came out of him like the heat off someone with fever. Every time he said no trouble, no more trouble, and he kept saying that, I could sense trouble, she said, I could feel my clothes tautening on me as if someone were pulling them tight from behind. I wanted to die and I wanted to face up to him, but I couldn't do either, so I just sat there, God forgive me, nodding at what he said, thinking, sweet Jesus, is there a child moving inside me, was that a kick I felt in my belly the way I used to when one of you was starting to move and I would know if it was a boy or a girl from the kind of kick it was – I did – and I was always right, for I'd tell your father when he came home which it was going to be. He always laughed at that but he believed me. If I said it was a girl, his face would always brighten more, for he thought with a girl it was an even bigger miracle, though that doesn't mean he didn't want any of you boys. He was just like that.

Was I at school the day Burke came in to talk to her? Even long after she told me about it, I convinced myself that I had been home that day and had heard his voice. The velvety crooning of pigeons from Freddie Campbell's shed, three doors up, used to bring sleep around me in the summer afternoons. We fancied we were experts on the pigeons, called them by their various names – fantails, ringers, homers, doves — and daily watched them flutter in circles above the roofs before they settled on the shed's corrugated tin slope. The seed they fed on and their blue-and-white droppings, the white a dry flare, the blue like an eye in the flare's head, were spattered all over the back yards in a harmless carnage. Was it on such an afternoon Burke had come in, while I lay there drowsing? It wasn't so, but I wanted it to be so. It happened in December, 1957, when I was still at school; but it was four years later, when I was starting at university, before she told me. And then, I think, it was only because I was going away to France for the summer vacation and she had this notion that I might never come back, or get killed in an accident. It was the night before I left. My father had gone out to see his brother Phonsie, who was ill. I was beginning to believe that she didn't mind so much my knowing what I did, was more assured of my silence, no matter what I knew.

There has to be an end to it, Burke had said, a complete end, a real finish. What was he meaning to say? she had asked him. Oh, Burke had replied, a separation from all that grief, a walking away from it, a settling. Look at your father, he told her, dying with two deaths on his conscience and both of them the wrong man. Look at Katie and her shattered marriage, and her child left without a father and the father living a double life out there in exile. Look at Frank, your husband, living in silence, believing his family disgraced by an informer and unwilling to talk about what he had had to suffer all those years with his children around him asking questions and other people wondering about him — wondering why he had been let go that night the young fella found the gun. He had fixed that himself, Burke claimed, for he didn't want to see Frank take any more, and he knew he was not involved in anything. Is that why you beat my wee'uns in front of him? she asked him in outrage. Is that why you left him black and blue to the waist? Sure he had to do that in front of the others, he said, the Special Branch from Belfast, else it would have looked strange, and if *they* had taken over, Frank would have been a long time in gaol. It took some effort on his part to persuade them Frank was harmless. But he was telling her now that he was sorry about it and sorry about that other incident when he got the young lad in trouble over the stone-throwing. But sure didn't the young fella come back at him through the Bishop? A clever wee lad that. But the poison was spreading to him and his sisters and brothers as well. Isn't it about time it was all stopped? Did nobody want free of it? Why had it to go on and on and on?

Well, she told me, she let him know in quick order why. Injustice. The police themselves. Dirty politics. It's grand to say let it stop to people who have been the victims of it. What were they supposed to do? Say they're sorry they ever protested and go back to being unemployed, gerrymandered, beaten up by every policeman who took the notion, gaoled by magistrates and judges who were so vicious that it was they who should be gaoled, and for life, for all the harm they did and all the lives they ruined? He had no answer to that. Just sat there with his head down, sighing every so often. And then he asked her if Frank knew, and was she going to tell him? And she told him that was between her and her husband, and if anyone else intervened, there'd be more trouble on that account than there ever was before.

What trouble? I asked her. What would she do? Christ in heaven knew what she could do, for what power had she, but she'd let them think she could do something or would do something. She was bluffing, like we learned to do at poker, I realised, and admired her but wondered how she could keep it up. Everybody was caged in. It was almost tidy.

At first, she hardly moved, she said, but she was terrified. There was Burke, standing in the kitchen, his peaked cap in his hand, his uniform black, black, with its shine of leather belt and holster, his gun strapped in by a thong, his baton adjusted at an angle. Did she mind if he removed his cap? If he sat down? There were one or two things on his mind he had to tell her, ask her about and thought it better to do it during the day when Frank was at work. All right, Ma'am? He did take off his cap and sat down, placing the cap on his knee, swinging the baton around a little until he was comfortable. He was so big he blocked most of the light from the window behind him. Nor could she see his face properly, for it was in half-darkness.

The door had been open and she had heard the quiet knock and had called on whomever it was to come in and there he was. Her immediate impulse was to shout at him to leave, but she had no voice. For a moment she thought there might have been an accident, someone dead or maimed, your father drowned at work, for he was in the water these days, pulling on hawsers attached to the ships, or working high on the dry dock and balancing on gangplanks that he thought were too narrow and too frail and gave him vertigo. They were stripping down one of the battleships from the mothball fleet that was left over from the war. Then she thought it might be one of us, run over by a coal lorry or kicked by one of those loose horses the tinkers left to wander in the back field. But the minute he spoke, she knew it was none of that. Even then, she was left looking for her voice, trying to wet her mouth with her spittle so that she could ease the soreness of her suddenly-dry throat.

Burke said he knew about Katie's daughter, Maeve, that she had married and had had a child over there in England. It had set him thinking, he claimed, of all that had happened since the days Katie had been married herself. It was a terrible pity the way things turned out sometimes, for that could have been a happy marriage, and neither Katie nor Maeve would have been left without a husband on the one hand, and without a father on the other, if all that old trouble had not come up again. Politics destroyed people's lives in this place, he said. People were better not knowing some things, especially the younger people, for all that bother dragged on them all their lives, and what was the point? He said, she told me, that he wanted to retire soon and he had

had enough of it himself. Wanted to make his peace with it, but it was hard for him too. He still remembered his friend Billy Mahon, who had started out with him all those decades ago in the police force in the days of the shootings after the Treaty. Those were bad years, he said, the early twenties. Northern Ireland had had a cruel birth. And Billy Mahon had had a cruel death, and he wasn't the man responsible for the death of her father's friend that night outside the newspaper office. Your father, he told her, was a hard man and a clever man. He had got off for that killing and they couldn't get him on anything after that, he was so careful. My mother said her voice had come back at that; she told him, she said, that it wasn't for want of trying, and Sergeant Burke had just nodded and said all right, they had got back at him by using McIlhenny, Katie's husband, as he was later to be. McIlhenny was their man. He had given them the tip-off. But it was too dangerous to have him brand Eddie directly with that, so they had found a way to let it leak, as if by accident, that Eddie had done it. Larry McLaughlin was the fall guy for that; he thought he had picked up incriminating evidence against Eddie from a friendly source within the police. It was double-cross on double-cross; and it had worked. So when Eddie was shot, they were going to let her father know the mistake he had made but instead they had been told to keep their man, McIlhenny, in place, as a kind of sleeper and they had done that until the time, after he had married Katie, someone had found out and told. He often wondered who that was; for he had had to get McIlhenny out and the man was in a terrible state, for he knew he'd never be able to come back and he didn't want to leave his young wife and didn't know if she'd be allowed to come out after him, if they'd tell her. Was it your father, he asked, that forbade her to go out to Chicago? Pregnant as she was, only a few months married? Was McIlhenny still alive? And was it true, as he had heard it, that he had married again and was still living there and never had any contact with anyone?

I wanted to tell her it was all right now, that it was all

over. But it wasn't. She hadn't told me about McIlhenny and her; she hadn't told me how much she knew, or my father knew, when they got married. I know you went out with McIlhenny, Mother. I know you kept that from my father.

I imagined talking to her like this, rehearsing conversations I would never have. 'What *you* don't know doesn't hurt *you*,' I would say. 'What I don't know and you won't tell, that does hurt me. That's what's happening here. If you loved me more or knew how much I loved you and him, then you would say everything. How can you not know? I'd do anything, *anything*, to help you if you'd let me.' But was that true, that she would tell everything if she loved me more? If she knew there was *something* more, but didn't know what it was, wasn't that worse for her, wasn't that what would stop her saying anything more to me? Imagining something, like the way Eddie died, like who was there, like what exactly had happened, that was maybe worse than having just the one set of facts, the one story that cancelled all the others, the one truth she could tell. But everyone who had been there was dead or in exile or silenced one way or the other. And how did I know I had been told the truth? Shouldn't I just ask her? What did you know, Mother, when you married my father? What did he know? When did you tell each other? Why did you silence me, over and over? Don't you remember the roses? You knew what that was about; so did he. Why didn't you tell me? If you had really cared, you would have. Can't you see what you are doing, even now, telling me all that Burke said and still not telling me anything I didn't find out for myself, not telling me about you and my father, you and McIlhenny, but letting me know about everything else?

She was looking at me. I smiled at her.

CHAPTER SIX

PEOPLE IN SMALL PLACES

June 1958

Once, I said to my mother, Katie had told me a strange story that her husband, McIlhenny, had told her. It was soon after she got pregnant with Maeve. It was when McIlhenny got a summer job as a conductor on the Lough Swilly buses that plied between Derry and Donegal on the Inishowen route – Derry, Burnfoot, Fahan, Buncrana, Malin, Carndonagh, Gleneely, Moville, Derry – with lots of stops in between at houses, cottages, by-ways. Did she know that story? Did she remember it?

'I remember the moral of the story,' she said, 'as he told it. Pity he didn't remember it himself.'

I told it to her again, probing for a reaction. She sat there very calmly, letting me do it.

One of McIlhenny's regular passengers, every Wednesday, was a man from Malin town, right at the tip of the Inishowen peninsula. He was called Sean. He'd come on the bus always carrying a small, brown attaché case, much bruised, in his huge hand. He kept it on his knee all during the bus-ride, in and out. There was nothing in it but one baby sock. McIlhenny had nodded to himself, Katie had said, in the satisfied way he had, when he announced this, and carefully lifted a strand of his black hair that always fell over his face when he nodded, and placed it back. Oh, he had a helmet of real black hair, she told me. As for Sean, that was it. Nothing else. One baby sock. When McIlhenny was asked how he knew that, he had said that Sean had opened the case once and shown him the sock, saying, 'Take a look at that. The day I find its match, I stop all this travelling.'

Well, it seemed that Sean had lost his infant daughter,

209

years before. She had died in the fever hospital in Derry. Was brought in of an afternoon and was dead by teatime. Sean had collected all her belongings that evening, but one sock went missing. He was still trying to find it. He went to the hospital every day and sat in the waiting room and the nurses would come in and tell him they were sorry, they had looked, but could not find it. They humoured him. There was no point in pretending they had found its match because, first, they had never seen the one in the suitcase and, second, Sean would have said no anyway, to any sock, that it wasn't the match. And there are lots like him, McIlhenny had said. If you saw what was in the luggage that's carried on that bus, you'd wonder what world you lived in. Country people are strange, he had said. They take everything personally, even accidents. If there's been a disaster, they always find some blame somewhere, in someone, often enough in themselves. Sean from Malin believed his child could not enter Paradise until he, Sean, had collected everything belonging to it. It was a way of blaming himself for the child's death. McIlhenny was asked what colour the sock was. Yellow, with a red stripe around the rim of it. He had said that the worst punishment of all was the one Sean of Malin had created for his child – not being able to let it die properly, getting it caught between this world and the next. The air of Donegal, of all Ireland, was full of such people, he had claimed, because of our bad history. Look at Lord Leitrim over in the valley of Glenveagh. An evil bastard, who cleared the valley of its people and got shot for it. Be sure, he had no rest. He still rode that road every night as dusk was falling, up to the hedge where they shot him from, a figure on a horse, like a silhouette, with a broad-brimmed hat and a cloak. The horse itself made no noise. It galloped along until it neared the spot in the hedge, and, then, for a second or two, you could hear its hoofbeats drumming. As you heard these, the figure on the horse vanished for an instant; then when you looked up the road, there it was again, gliding away into the darkness in absolute silence. And

Lord Leitrim and his kind would be like that until the Day of Judgement: never alive, never dead, just shadows in the air.

I imagined McIlhenny standing at the door, across from the driver, as the bus bucketed along the road outside Moville and the lough spreading open below Greencastle, Redcastle, Quigley's Point, up to the silent reaches of Culmore where my father had rowed Liam and me across the river. My mother said she remembered him singing an emigrant's song about Creeslough, a small town I had never seen, tucked into the coast of North Donegal, on the road that led into the Irish-speaking districts of Ranafast and Loughanure, where I wished I could go and learn to speak properly the language I had mutilated before my mother and father.

So what was the moral of the story? I asked her.

Oh, she answered, it was that people in small places make big mistakes. Not bigger than the mistakes of other people. But that there is less room for big mistakes in small places. She smiled ironically.

'As he knows now,' she said, 'as we all do.'

CRAZY JOE AND MOTHER

October 1958

Joe took to visiting my mother regularly after his release
from the asylum. My father, when he came in from work,
would swear under his breath if Joe was there, nattering on,
his appearance still unchanged, grotesque and fresh at the
same time. She was the only one Joe would now talk to at
any length. What does she find to say to him? my father
would wonder aloud to us. How can she stand that jabbering,
all that nonsense he talks? Joe would not stay long after my
father appeared. He'd stand up, put on his hat, doff it again
in a sweep to my mother and declare, 'Tempus is fugiting,
my dear. I must be off.'

But he was there quite often in the afternoons when I
came in from school, sitting there on the sofa, talking into
the air, rising up every so often to gesticulate or adopt a
pose, while my mother leaned back in the armchair, seem-
ingly attentive to the multi-voiced drama Joe was enacting
before her, full of memories or fantasies from his stay in the
asylum. Two or three of us would stay in to watch and listen,
our schoolbags thrown under the table, as Joe cavorted and
performed.

His abiding memory of his time in the asylum was
of beatings from male nurses, of being plunged in baths of
freezing water if he irritated them in any way. To live with
this condition of his was, he said, the great connubium of
his infelicity – the condition of being sane married to the
condition of being mad; the knowledge that he was mad
married to the knowledge that he was sane; knowing that
he was harmless but that his condition made others harmful.
And people thought he wasn't married! He was as unhappily
married as anyone he knew. It was a favour, he said, to any

couple to put an end to that condition. Wasn't that so? When he tipped the wink, he told my mother, tipped the wink to you-know-who about the other you-know-who, look at the trouble that got him into, but look at the trouble it got him and her out of, and wasn't he right? Wasn't he right? Wasn't that so, missis? He wasn't mad.

Then he would weep, and my mother would rouse herself to tell him it was all right now, he was out of there, he wouldn't be going back; it was all over. But Joe would shake his head and say it wasn't, his relations would put him back, no one could stand him around, he was too hard to live with, but why was it so, what had he done?

But soon he would be smiling again and nodding at us as we moved about. I felt sorry for him too, but her sympathy for him angered me. Why couldn't she show the same interest in us? In my father?

One day, as my father came in and was washing his hands at the scullery sink, Joe stood up, swept his hat on and off in the usual way, and said in front of us all, 'But for all that, missis, for all that, I never told them your story. Family secrets are family secrets. Sure they might have come down here and told himself out there.' The noise of the water running in the scullery stopped. My mother put a finger to her lips.

'Now, Joe,' she said.

'On my oath, missis. The crown jewels are safe with me. No point in telling a secret, is there? What good's a secret if too many people know it?'

My father came in, rubbing his arms and hands on a towel, an inquiring look on his face. Joe fled, almost bowing as he backed down the hall.

'What was he talking about?' my father asked.

My mother dismissed it. Joe, raving as ever. His head was scrambled worse every time he came out of the asylum. Perhaps it was the way she put her head down as she answered my father, perhaps it was just the accumulation of all that Joe had said – but I suddenly knew.

Ah, God. Now I knew. All of it, the final melancholy. Your last secret was with Joe, Mother. In Crazy Joe's loose keeping, locked and unlocked in the asylum at Gransha.

MOTHER

November 1958

My mother, as if she knew what Crazy Joe had made known to me, became hostile. She kept up a low-intensity warfare. No, Gerard would bring in the coal. No, Eamon would go to the butcher's. No, Deirdre would make her a cup of tea. No, she didn't think I should go to the pictures and anyway she didn't have the threepence I needed. Above all, no, I wasn't to go over to Katie's to get messages for her; one of the others would do that. Katie had told her Liam was quicker at it anyway. I'd be better occupied if I did some school work, I'd been slacking a lot lately. I'd the Junior Certificate examination this year, and she expected distinctions in every subject. *Ten* distinctions? Irish, English, History, French, Greek, Latin, Geography, Geometry, Mathematics, Art. She counted them off on her fingers. And then there was the All-Ireland Religious Knowledge examination after that. Liturgy, Doctrine, Bible. I had to do well in that too. She kept her face very severe as she ticked all these off.

'OK,' I said, 'Ten distinctions.'

When I got nine – with a pass in Art – she asked what happened to the promise of ten. I told her I broke it. I was joking. She was not.

'So you did. So you did,' she replied.

I scored high in the Religious Knowledge test, but that wasn't good enough either.

'You could have come first in Ireland if you had tried harder,' she accused.

She persisted, right into the winter. On All Souls' Night, we went in and out of the cathedral, saying set prayers for the repose of one soul after another. We used to believe, when younger, that a falling star in the winter sky was a soul released from fire into paradise, a flash into eternity. This year, as always, we were to pray especially for Una, and after her all the dead relations – grandparents, Eddie, Ena – then all the souls in purgatory who were close to final salvation. We exited after each set of prayers, re-entered for the next. She saw Brendan Moran and me talking to two girls outside. At home, later that evening, she told me she had seen me behaving disgracefully in the church grounds, that it made her blush to think that gom was her son, chasing round like that with young girls on a holy night such as this. It would be a while before she would see me staying out at night again.

Fuck this, I thought. What's she at? Challenging me? I said nothing.

My father was visibly annoyed and puzzled, but wasn't going to say anything to her in front of us. He was fifty. He looked older. When he was showing me how to box, how to move my feet and angle my body, and held my fist in his hand to fold the thumb into the centre of my palm, his hand felt smaller than it had at the beginning of the year when he had handselled us all with a shilling each for the New Year and shaken us all in turn by the hand while the cathedral bells rang out in the frost.

My mother was increasingly distant from everyone; slowly slipping out of our grasp, slick with hostility. Her anger stayed in her eyes when she was speaking, but when she was silent an empty panic took its place. I stole for her a golden iris from a flower stall in Chamberlain Street and walked into the kitchen, handed it to her and said to her, 'Don't worry any more. I'll never say a word. Don't worry about it. It's all past.'

She took the flower with its three heads and three petals on each.

'Look,' she said, tearing the petals off, one at a time, and letting them drop on the floor:

'If you want to, you can tell,'

One petal dropped off.

'If you don't, that's just as well.'

Another swirled on to the linoleum.

*'Get it over, get it done,
Father, lover, husband, son.'*

She laughed coldly and threw the remains on the floor, folded her arms across her breast and rocked back and forth, humming tunelessly. Her hair was greying at the side, above her ear.

I picked up the flowers and the petals and tossed them into the bin out in the yard. She was nearly gone from me. I remembered how she had put her hand to her heart the day I had destroyed the roses and realised how youthful her face had been then. Looking through the window, I could see her still swaying back and forth, and my heart went out to her even as I wished I could love her in the old way again. But I could only grieve for not being able to; and grieve the more that she could not love me like that any more either. The air smarted with rain.

'Did you say something to her? Did something happen? my father asked me.

'No. I said nothing,' I answered, feeling I was really telling the truth that mattered, although he couldn't know that.

He sighed. 'I don't know why she's taken against you so much. Don't be upset. She can't help it, God look to her.'

She took to the lobby window again. But she disliked anyone standing with her there to talk, most especially me. There she was with her ghosts. Now the haunting meant something new to me – now I had become the shadow. Everything bore down on her. She got smaller, more intense, her features sealed into no more than two or three expressions. In addition, she fell silent. My father persuaded her to let the doctor come and see her. 'Her nerves have got the better of her,' he announced and prescribed sedatives that she refused to take. 'Don't bring that fool near me again,' she told my father.

DANCE

December 1958

A firm called Birmingham Sound Reproducers opened a
factory on Bligh's Lane, just a couple of hundred yards away
from us. They employed a lot of men. It was strange to see
men coming home from work at the same time as the
women from the few shirt factories that had survived. It
changed the whole pattern of movement in the neighbourhood. Also, many people got record-players cheap, direct
from the factory; the street got noisier, especially in summer
when the doors and windows were left open, and the music
blared out. We got one too, and my father played the same
three records – collections of arias, mostly from Italian opera
– every night when he came home from work. As the arias
streamed out from the green-and-grey box, he would close
his eyes and lean back, rapt with the sound of Gigli above
all others. My mother would sit, unmoved, perhaps not even
hearing it, although now and then I thought I saw her
looking at him sadly as though he were a young boy who
didn't know the trouble that lay ahead of him. My favourite
was an aria sung by Björling; Orpheus having turned round
too soon and lost Eurydice – *Che farò senza Euridice?* It
wound out from the black disc in long sorceries of sound. I
would sit beside the machine sometimes, facing her, and it
was then as though the music was winding out of me, a
lamentation for the loss of her.

With the new record-players available, somebody had
the idea that there should be social evenings with music and
dancing in the local Ashfield Hall, at the foot of Tyrconnell
Street. People of all ages came, every second Tuesday. Usually,
I sat in sidelong-eyed discomfort during the dancing and
singing in case some girl, even my sister Eilis, might ask me

to dance. But I need not have worried. Instead, Crazy Joe came along, still wielding his walking stick, and sat on the bench beside me in the darkest corner of the local hall. Joe was invited to nothing and he came to everything – weddings, wakes, birthday parties, anniversaries, dances. He stared at the dancers moving round the floor space cleared by piling the benches at both ends of the hall. His false teeth slid in and out, a smile in mid-air, a smile in his face, alternately. The suction of his mouth remained audible above the noise of the recorded dance music – and of the crowd. A girl from Cable Street approached and smiled in my direction. I bared my teeth at her, thinking I must look like Joe, a smiling non-smile semaphoring in the semi-darkness of the low-lit hall. But she moved away again. I wished I could dance, but it wasn't only dancing that was the problem. There was touching and talking to girls and being watched by the older people.

'Stay away from the women, boy. Don't let their smiles fool you.'

Now he's going to say, 'Stick to football,' I thought, feeling nauseated.

'Stick to your books,' he advised, clapping me on the bare knee and squeezing it a little. I constricted my body inward, away from him.

'Filthy lot!'

'What do you mean, filthy?'

'Lot is fate. Once you see that, you see everything. Why is everyone so stupid? You've a lot of books to stick to, I can see that, if you can see the pun, though I'm sure you don't. Here comes another one of those women. Tell her to get lost. I want to talk to you.'

But, whoever she was, she was not interested. She passed us by without a glance. Liam was dancing. He was waving his arms and clicking his fingers. Envy sprang like a trap inside me. Joe touched my knee again, very lightly. Teeth in, teeth out. Suction noises. His right hand shifted back and forth on the curve of his stick that he kept perpendicular on the floor. His other hand strayed by his side.

'Sexual heat. That's all drums are for. It'd make you sick, that music. Should be banned.'

I could see my mother and Katie with some other women seated in a circle around a table to the side of the platform where the music was playing. Katie was dabbing her eyes, and my mother was bent in close to her, talking and patting her bare arm. I wondered what had upset Katie. My father sat down the hall on a bench, upright, alone, although he seemed to be smiling a little. Most of the other men of his age were in a corner of the hall, round a table, drinking. I could hear their talk coming and going in waves: 'Oh listen, says I, says I, listen to this . . . ' 'An' I turned round and said not you nor any one of your family ever could . . . ' Joe stopped his sucking and turned to me, his face calm with madness.

'Here's a conundrum. There's a place where a man died but lived on as a ghost, and where another man lived as a ghost but died as a man, and where another man would have died as a man but ran away to live as a ghost. Where would that place be?'

He put his hand on my knee again. I ignored it. He rubbed my knee as though it were the crook of his walking stick. I looked at his hand moving on me. The noise in the hall was terrible. His teeth slid out as he stared me in the face.

'Where? Where?'

'I don't know. You tell me.'

'Don't know? Me tell you? I could tell you anywhere. Egypt? Brazil? The Atlantic Ocean? The back of beyond? In the Bible? C'mon. Guess, you scut. You know damn well.'

He rubbed my knee vigorously and at that I was lifted clean off the chair and planted on the ground. My father was holding my shirt at the back of the neck and staring furiously at Joe.

'Don't you ever lay a hand on him again, y'hear that?'

Joe quailed and put one hand up across his face, saying

nothing. He sat there like that, the other hand still gripping his stick. People were looking in our direction. My father pushed me ahead of him.

'Stay away from Joe; he's sick in the head. What were you sitting there with him for? Go and dance or talk with people your own age. Go on.'

He pushed me forward, and I wandered ahead of him, seeing my mother and Katie turn round to look down the floor, hearing my father resume his seat behind me, seeing Joe as we left him, arm across his face and his wild eyes staring. A girl touched my arm.

'Y'want to dance?'

I moved gratefully to the floor with her, wanting to hold her tight in my arms.

The next day, my mother also told me to stay away from Crazy Joe. I spent too much time with him, she claimed, and he was not normal. I was never to let him touch me. He was odd. You mean he's queer? I asked. She shook her head almost in disbelief at the word. Then she shook her head again.

'God forgive me, God forgive what I have done,' she wailed.

222

BIRTHDAY GIFT

May 1959

It wasn't just that she was trapped by what had happened. She was trapped by my knowing it. It must be shame, I decided. She's paralysed by shame. She was ashamed of what she had done to my father. She was ashamed, I knew it. Every time she saw me, she felt exposed, even though I made it clear I would never say anything and even tried to make it clear that I understood why she had behaved so. But I couldn't wholly understand, not without knowing more. I wanted to ask her if she had loved McIlhenny at any time, really loved him. But I was afraid she might say she still loved him, or even that she loved him for the years in between, when she first went out with him, through his leaving her and marrying Katie, through her fingering him, with Joe's help, as the informer, through her tipping him off and seeing him flee and vanish to Chicago, through Katie's grief, and finally through her meeting my father four years later and realising what Eddie had meant to him and his family. I didn't want to hear that she had loved him for all of that time or for any part of it, even though I knew there must be some truth in it. What, finally, did she not know when she stood with my father at the altar-rail to be married? That her father had ordered Eddie's execution? Was that all she didn't know? And what did he know? Just that his brother was an informer who had been shot? Yet there were all those years since their marriage in 1935. All those stories, hints, all that cover-up about Eddie having got away and disappeared. Did he not recognise that the story of Eddie and the story of McIlhenny were so close? How could he have missed the connection, how could he not have seen that one was the imprint of the other? Or did he know and hold in his pain, his suspicions, for saying it out loud would destroy everything, make their marriage impossible?

Sergeant Burke died, and his priest-sons concelebrated the Requiem Mass for him in the cathedral. The Bishop attended the funeral.

'How dare he do that!' hissed my mother.

She wouldn't listen to us tell her that the police and the priests were always in cahoots with one another. No theories like that for her. It was personal. Everything was personal. I understood that. It had to be, when everything that was precious to her was so bound up with betrayal.

I asked her once what she would like for her birthday.

'Just for that day,' she answered, 'just for that one day, the seventeenth of May, to forget everything. Or at least not to be reminded of it. Can you give me that?'

I didn't reply.

'Why don't you go away?' she asked me. 'Then maybe I could look after your father properly for once, without your eyes on me.'

I told her I would. I'd go away, after university. That would be her birthday gift, that promise. She nodded. I moved away just as she put out her hand towards me.

MY FATHER

June 1961

Staying loyal to my mother made me disloyal to my father. In case I should ever be tempted to tell him all I knew, I stayed at arm's length from him and saw him notice but could say nothing to explain. I went away to university in Belfast, glad to be free of the immediate pressures of living there, sorry to have so mishandled everything that I had created a distance between my parents and myself that had become my only way of loving them. So, I celebrated all the anniversaries: of all the deaths, all the betrayals – for both of them – in my head, year after year, until, to my pleasure and surprise, they began to become confused and muddled, and I wondered at times had I dreamed it all.

Hauntings are, in their way, very specific. Everything has to be exact, even the vaguenesses. My family's history was like that too. It came to me in bits, from people who rarely recognised all they had told. Some of the things I remember, I don't really remember. I've just been told about them so now I feel I remember them, and want to the more because it is so important for others to forget them. Someone told me how my father, the night his parents were buried, was found lying down in the back shed of that house on the High Street where they had lived, among the coal sacks and the chopped wood, crying unstoppably. I imagined it and believed it, but when I looked at him again, I wondered: was that my father?

My father. He would have loved to have been educated. When I came down from Belfast the night I got my degree, I came into a kitchen crammed with people and chatter. I'd had a few drinks and was feeling light, so as I came through the door, and as they looked up expectantly, I was about to put on an act of despair and pretend I'd failed, when I saw my father behind the door getting off his chair, his face grey, his legs leaden. The rafters came swooping down again, the cloud above the Atlantic nudged the light into rays and I was looking up at him as he straightened. At once I said, 'I got it. A First.' His huge hand held my shoulder for a second and he smiled.

'A First,' he said and sat down. 'A First,' he whispered to himself, his head down as everybody else began to talk again and my mother nodded at him and said, 'He's – we've been waiting since six for that news. What kept you? It's one in the morning.'

'I had a drink or two in Belfast.'

'A drink or two!' they all echoed, laughing.

'I'd have a drink myself if I didn't have to work in the morning.' He came from behind the door. 'But I'll sleep well tonight.'

He went upstairs. He never took a drink in his life. I've reconstructed his vigil behind the door in that noisy room a hundred times since, just as I reconstructed his life out of the remains of the stories about his dead parents, his vanished older brother, his own unknowing and, to me, beloved silence. Oh, father.

The man behind the door, the boy weeping in the coal shed, the walk down that dusty road, the ruined rose bed, the confession in the church, his dead, betrayed brother – was that all? In a whole lifetime? How bitterly did he feel or was he saddened into quietness? How much did he know or not know?

I remembered one night, long before I knew anything, we were all listening to a boxing match on BBC radio between the British heavyweight champion Bruce Woodcock and a Czechoslovak miner called Josef Baksi. My father, of course, knew something about boxing, and retained an interest in it

226

even though he said the sport sickened him. This was a terrible fight. Woodcock took a pulverising beating but stayed on his feet the whole way through the twelve rounds. The commentator was screaming as though someone were standing on his neck; the noise of the crowd seemed to swell the fabric on the radio's speaker. My father listened as though he had a gun in his back.

'Stop the fight,' he said to the radio every so often. 'Stop the fight.'

At one point he stood up and switched it off and lit a John Player's Navy Cut cigarette in the ensuing silence and smoked it until the untapped ash broke over his knuckles. Then he switched on again. It was the last round. Woodcock was being driven all over the ring. Then it was over.

'Brave but stupid,' he said, and went out first to the back yard and swept it, and then into the coal shed and broke the great shale pieces into black diamonds and gleaming ricochets, and hauled out tree blocks and broke them into gnarled sticks while the shed shook with the blows. I came out to look but he shooed me away without turning around. My mother shushed us all up to bed. When she put her finger to her lips, I knew I wasn't imagining his sorrow, but I couldn't fathom it. I lay awake all night and heard him go out in the morning at six. I crept to the lobby window and watched him cross the back lane and go down the New Road with his lunch bag in his hand. But it was no help. I could decipher nothing and was so tired at school that day that I fell asleep twice.

'Shush,' said Brother Collins, 'we mustn't talk too loud. We might waken him. Maybe we should croon a little lullaby. One, two, three.'

His face, when I opened my eyes, was a millimetre away, but I saw only my father. And the blows, when they came, shook in last night's shed and were scarcely felt.

AFTER

July 1971

I told no one else, not even Liam, what I knew and hoped my mother would notice I was keeping a pact with her. But she seemed to pay no attention. What we both knew separated us. I grieved for her and for him. I grieved for myself. I was losing her. She kept her lips compressed, looking more severe, more like her father with his Roman stoniness, as the years passed. As with my father, I watched on the dates of the various anniversaries that I thought she must remember and mourn or celebrate in a year. The beginning and end of her relationship with McIlhenny, the death of Eddie, the birth of Maeve, the disappearance of McIlhenny, marrying my father, Una's death, her mother's, her father's death, our births, Maeve's marriage. While my father, ignorant of McIlhenny, had some of these things and perhaps the feud, his parents' death, Ena's death – they were more intertwined than he knew, more so than she had ever wanted. Perhaps they didn't celebrate them; perhaps the only way they – especially she – could go on was by forgetting, forgetting. Katie stopped, like someone frozen in time; she pursued nothing any more, simply economised with what she had and greeted Maeve's children, four of them, as they arrived, and saw the whole connection soften towards them and towards Marcus, until it seemed as though, on their infrequent visits, they had always been part of the extended family, still a little exotic but no longer beyond tolerance.

Was nothing ever said, in all those years afterwards, as we grew up, as their marriage mutated slowly around the secrets that she kept in a nucleus within herself and that he sensed, even though he also thought he was free of the one secret he knew, since he had told us, false as it was? I would watch them together as they aged. She was less haunted, it seemed, than before; he was still anxious with the air of someone whose anxiety was never focused. He knew something lay beyond him but he had no real wish to reach for it.

Maybe it was wise for him, for the whole marriage had been preserved by his not allowing the poison that had been released over all these years, as from a time-release capsule, to ever get to him in a lethal dose. I would have readily died rather than say anything to him, or insinuate anything before her, about that last big mistake that so filled the small place they lived in. Of course, Joe did not go to the IRA with his information about McIlhenny. He would not have known where to go. He went to my mother. I knew this without any doubt. It was as if she had told me outright. It was she who brought Joe to my grandfather and had Joe tell what he saw that night of the eighth of July 1926 when he saw McIlhenny get out of Burke's police car in the small hours of the morning. That's when Grandfather realised for sure the mistake he had made with Eddie. But even then, my mother didn't know the full story of Eddie's death – just that he had been executed in error. But not on her father's orders. That she couldn't have known, else she would not have been so upset that evening I was staying with her dying father and she had come down so distressed, saying Eddie's name. What she knew was bad enough. McIlhenny, her sister's husband, the man she had once loved – maybe still loved – and who had ditched her, was an informer. Now she was informing on him. But rather than sentencing him to death, perhaps she was the one who then went and told him his cover was blown, that he had better get out. And then she had married my father, closing herself in forever, haunted forever.

Her small figure at the turn of the stair; when I had left home, that was how I remembered her. Haunted, haunted. Now that everything had become specific, it was all the more insubstantial. How I had wanted to know what it was

229

that plagued her, then to become the plague myself. There had been a time when, once a year, she placed a bet on the Aintree Grand National horse race. Having a wee flutter, she called it. Every year she backed the horse that was drawn number thirteen. One year, I placed the two-shilling bet for her and she won. I raced back to the bookmakers for her winnings and brought the money home to her. She took it and smiled and gave me a hug.

'You have the luck for me,' she had said.

That was a long time ago.

I felt it was almost a mercy when my mother suffered a stroke and lost the power of speech, just as the Troubles came in October 1968. I would look at her, sealed in her silence, and now she would smile slightly at me and very gently, almost imperceptibly, shake her head. I was to seal it all in too. Now we could love each other, at last, I imagined. Now we could have the luck for each other.

We choked on CS gas fired by the army, saw or heard the explosions, the gunfire, the riots moving in close with their scrambled noises of glass breaking, petrol-bomb flashings, isolated shouts turning to a prolonged baying and the drilled smashing of batons on riot shields. Now the television was on all the time, but she looked at it without watching it. We begged her not to stand at the window, where she did watch, when the army was firing or when the IRA was sniping. She was not deterred at all by any of this from her patrolling of the stairs, the lobby, the fireside, where a tile surround had replaced the old range and made the threshold of the fire naked and banal.

My father would sit with her at times, holding her hand, watching the television, both of them listening to the noise outside – shouts, occasional rifle fire, now and then the jump and boom of a bomb going off down town. They were on their own in the house by this time. Everyone had moved out, gone away, got married; but we visited them often. I used to wonder what it did to them, watching and listening to the war outside. Twice the house was searched and badly damaged by British soldiers; Eamon was arrested and released; Gerard was batoned by the police during a riot. All through this, my father remained as silent as my mother. I imagined that, in her silence, in the way she stroked his hand, smiled crookedly at him, let him brush her hair, bowing her head obediently for him, she had told him and won his understanding. I could believe now, as I never had when a child, that they were lovers.

And suddenly, just before retirement, he had a heart attack. He lost his pension because he had flaked out a year too early. Now, as the war in the neighbourhood intensified, they both sat there in their weakness, entrapped in the noise from outside and in the propaganda noise of the television inside.

I visited for a weekend, arriving on a Friday evening. It had been a bad week. Two days before, a British soldier, hunkering on the front doorstep, with his blackened face, had been shot dead by an IRA sniper during a street search. Hearing the thud, my father had struggled out of his armchair and opened the door a fraction. He saw the man lying there, his face up, his mouth open. He shut the door quickly and they both listened to the roaring of the other soldiers, the door being kicked, scatterings of shots. He was still shaken when I arrived; then, a couple of hours later, there was a knock on the door. I opened it to a man who hesitantly took off his hat and asked if he could speak to someone in the house about the soldier who had been killed here on Wednesday. Before I could say anything, he added hastily that he was not army intelligence or police. He was the soldier's father. I invited him in. He introduced himself to my parents, told them he was from Yorkshire, a miner, and that his son, George, had been shot, he was told, at our doorstep. He wondered if anyone had seen what had happened. There was a silence. My parents looked at him. He knew, the

Yorkshireman said, he knew what people round here felt about the British soldiers. But this was his son. My father, who was struggling for breath these days, asked him if he wanted a cup of tea. I served it. My mother stared at him with the blankness that people who cannot speak can command.

Well, my father told the Englishman, his son had died instantly. He had heard the thud, not the shot. He had opened the door. The boy was lying there, looking quite peaceful. But he was dead, definitely dead.

'So he didn't suffer, didn't speak?' the miner asked.

No. They talked a little more, but there was not much to be said. The Englishman shook hands all round, we told him we were sorry for his trouble, he nodded, and left.

'Poor man,' said my father. 'I feel for him. Even if his son was one of those. It's a strange world.'

Not long after, a second heart attack killed my father in his sleep. My mother sat beside the coffin, dry-eyed, her hand on his folded hands, or on his brow; she would shiver slightly, as though at the cold of his body. He died the day a curfew was proclaimed by the army. The neighbourhood was closed between nine in the evening and nine the next morning while the street barricades were torn down. That night, I heard the armour coming in before I saw it from the upstairs window. The bulldozers came first, lifting and lowering their streaming jaws in the lamplight as they shunted the barricades aside. Behind them came the armoured personnel carriers, reconnoitring and stopping, nosing around the barricades and angling their seeing-lights down back lanes and side-streets. Other armoured trucks, with guns on top, with their yellow-and-white lights in front and their hard, high-pressure tyres, flashed their red-sashed sidelights and showed in their turnings glimpses of the avocado battle-dress of the soldiers who sat in facing rows within them.

I lay awake until dawn, when the noise of horse-hooves roused me to the window again. As though in a dream, I watched a young gypsy boy jog sedately through the scurf of debris astride a grey-mottled horse. Bareback, he held lightly to the horse's mane and turned out of sight in the direction the army had taken hours before, although it was still curfew. The clip-clop of the hooves echoed in the still streets after he had disappeared.

I went down the stairs to make tea. In the hallway, I heard a sigh and looked back to the lobby window. There was no shadow there. It must be my mother in her sleep, sighing, perhaps, for my father. It was her last sleep of the old world. By nine o'clock, curfew would be over. That evening we would take my father to the cathedral that hung in the stair window and she would climb to her bedroom in silence, pausing at the turn of the stairs to stare out at the spire under which, for that night, before the darkened altar, he so innocently lay.